THE TOMB

THE TOMB

THE PANTHERA LEGACY
BOOK TWO

W. MICHAEL GEAR

KATHLEEN O'NEAL GEAR

WOLFPACK
PUBLISHING
— EST 2013 —

ACKNOWLEDGMENTS

We would like to offer our sincere gratitude to the following scholars for the many lessons in religious studies and philosophy: Bruce W. Jones, Gary E. Kessler, L. Stafford Betty, Jacqueline Kegley, Norman Prigge, John Bash, Shigeo Kanda, and Donald Heinz. And though he can no longer hear us in this world, we also offer our heartfelt thanks to Dr. Charles W. Kegley. No more hiding the light under the bushel, Charles. We appreciate all of you.

ACKNOWLEDGMENTS

INTRODUCTION

There is an alternate story of the life of Jesus. It is a very *human* story, one that has been suppressed for nineteen centuries. Those of you who are not familiar with this story may find it disturbing. If so, you are not alone. The early Church fathers found the books that chronicled this story so menacing that they outlawed them, ordered them burned, and threatened with death anyone found copying them.

Remember that what follows is based on actual documents recovered from archaeological sites in the Middle East, or respected repositories of ancient literature, like the Vatican library.

Yeshua ben Miriam's story, that is, the story of Jesus, the son of Mary, as told in these books, is brilliant and tragic. It is the story of a man whose own family thought he was mad (Mark 3:21). It is the story of a man who met a violent end at the hands of Roman authorities. Nearly all of the ancient texts verify that Yeshua was crucified as the "King of the Jews." He was not, as many movies and books would have us believe, a meek man who spent his time spinning parables and healing the sick. Such a Jesus would have been a threat to no one. The historical Jesus *did* threaten and enrage people, from the priestly aristocracy in the Jerusalem temple to the Roman prefect who finally condemned him to be crucified.

He was a controversial figure. For many of you, this will be a controversial book.

Keep in mind that during the first and second centuries an immense variety of Christian beliefs and practices existed. There were numerous gospels.[1] It took three hundred years before the Church decided to organize an ecumenical council—the Council of Nicea in 325 C.E.—to dictate uniformity and outlaw all gospels that did not meet its narrow criteria of Truth.

The New Testament as we know it today was not finally settled on in the West until around the year 400.

Because the ancient accounts of the life of Jesus often conflict, we have used the archaeological record and the earliest documentary evidence to piece together this story. The documents include the traditional New Testament books, the Qumran and Nag Hammadi codices, as well as other literature that dates from roughly 50 C.E. to 250 C.E. These early documents are probably closer to the truth than the later, and much more spectacular, documents written in the late third and fourth centuries, or even later. We have footnoted the sources of the major events, especially those that are dramatically different from the traditional story of Jesus's life and the lives of those around him. There is a bibliography in the back of this book for those who want to see the sources with their own eyes. *We urge you to read the notes, as they provide detailed information on the historical events surrounding the life of Jesus, and those closest to him.*

Some of you will consider these documents to be a threat to your faith. We especially encourage those who do to press on and read them. Knowledge does not destroy faith. It does not take Jesus away. In fact, we believe it can give back the profound meaning to his life that has been lost over centuries of revisionism.

GLOSSARY

With one exception, Jerusalem, we use the correct historical names for biblical places and characters like Jesus, Mary, Joseph, and John—which means we use the names they would actually have been called by at the time. Many of the names are obvious. For example, Markos and Loukas were clearly the figures we know as "Mark" and "Luke." Bet Lehem and Bet Ani are "Bethlehem" and "Bethany." Other proper names, however, are not so obvious. Hopefully, this glossary will alleviate some of the confusion associated with the more unfamiliar names.

Please keep in mind that though scholars suspect some of the original gospels may have been written in Hebrew or Aramaic, the extant New Testament documents were written in the Greek language, which means the original Hebrew or Aramaic names of people like Yeshua (Jesus) and Yakob (James) were translated into Greek as Iesous and Iakobos.

Lastly, in Greek there is no sh sound, and in Hebrew and Aramaic there is no j sound. As well,

Hebrew and Aramaic are written almost entirely without vowels. These unique features of the languages have led to many spelling variations over time, as can be seen in the following.

- **Galilee:** In Hebrew it was referred to as the *Galil*. In the original Greek New Testament it was called the *Galilaian*.
- **James:** In Hebrew and Aramaic his name was *Ya'akov,* or *Yakob* (Jacob). In Greek it was *Iakobos,* and in Latin, *Iacomus,* which when translated into the Germanic spelling became *Jacomus,* then in Spanish *Jaime*. Finally, because the King James version translated it as *James* in 1611, it has remained *James* ever since in English translations.
- **Jerusalem:** Hebrew: *Yerushalaim*. Greek: *Ierosoluma*. We mention the Greek here only for the sake of historicity. From this point on, in the chapters set in the fourth century, you will read "Jerusalem." We have made this concession because we think the English name helps to better anchor English readers to the place and time.
- **Jesus**: His name was *Yeshua* in Hebrew, or in more formal situations—for example, in the Jerusalem Temple—*Yehoshua*. However, because the first-century dialect of Galilee dropped the final letter (*ayin*), Yeshua's Galilean friends, or those who were very close to him, probably called him by the name *Yeshu*. As well, early rabbinic

sources largely use *Yeshu* for "Jesus of Nazareth," and the Talmud *only* uses *Yeshu* for "Jesus of Nazareth." In Greek, his name was *Iesous,* or *Iesous Christos,* which we translate into English as "Jesus" or "Jesus Christ."

- **Jews:** Hebrew: *Yehudim.* Greek: *Ioudaiosoi.*
- **John:** The Hebrew is *Yohanan.* Greek: *Ioannes.*
- **Joseph:** Hebrew: *Yosep, Yosef,* or in more formal situations, *Yehosef.* In the Greek manuscripts there is a great deal of variance: *Ioses, Iose, Iosetos, Ioseph.* Many scholars believe that the form *Ioses* follows the Galilean pronunciation of the Hebrew *Yosep.*
- **Mary:** *Miriam* in Hebrew. In Aramaic it became *Maryam,* and in Coptic it was *Mariham.* The New Testament Greek gospels call her *Maria* or *Mariam.*
- **Matthew:** In Hebrew it is *Matthias, Mattiyahu, or Matya.* The Greek is *Maththaios.*

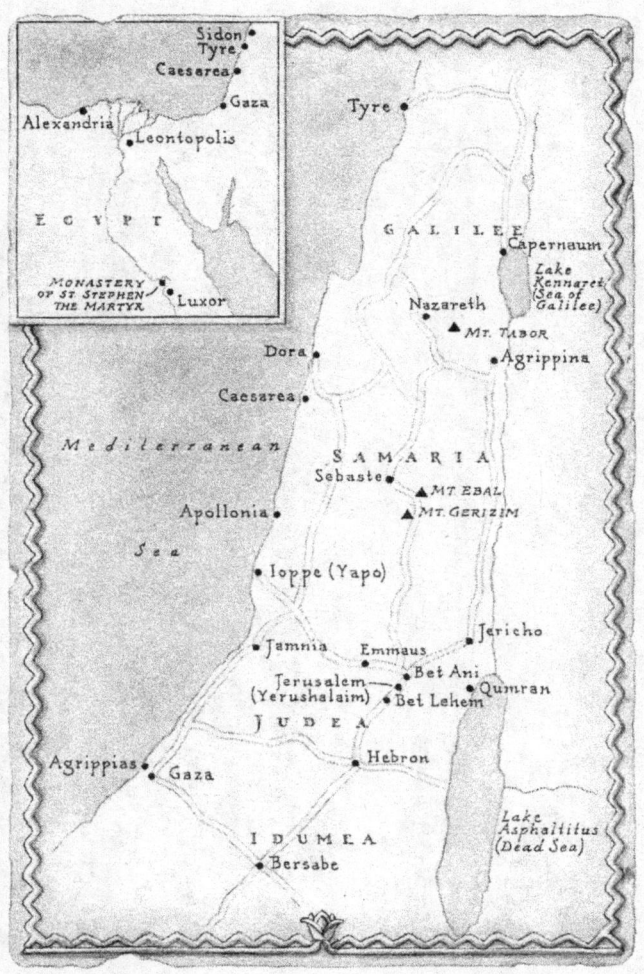

THE TOMB

1

As they rode over the last hill, the dark moonlit ocean came into view, and Zarathan heaved a sigh of relief. Seagulls squealed and soared on the cool sea breezes.

"How far now?" he asked.

Barnabas pulled up on the reins and came to a stop. "I'm not certain. None of this looks familiar."

"But we're about the right distance from Agrippias, aren't we?"

"Yes, but I don't see the pillar of rock and two humps of stone that the man spoke of, do you?"

Zarathan scanned the terrain. The outlines of the hills were clearly visible. Unfortunately, the vista resembled a vast plain of camelbacks dissected by rocky wadis. The line of white surf divided the worlds of land and water. Wave-washed beach gleamed in the evening light, but off to the east, behind the sullen line of cliffs, ridge after rocky ridge, each limned by crescent dunes, marched off into infinity.

"Perhaps we should camp on the beach and look in the morning when it's light," Barnabas suggested.

"Yes, good idea," Zarathan agreed. "If nothing else, we can dig clams and eat them raw."

Cyrus and Kalay rode up beside them. Cyrus had his curly black hair tucked behind his ears, which made his bearded face seem all the more hard and dangerous. He said, "Camping on the beach in the open makes me uneasy. Let's search for a better place."

Barnabas nodded. "Very well. You lead, Cyrus."

Cyrus kicked his horse into a slow walk and Barnabas and Zarathan plodded up the trail behind.

Occasional farmers and fishermen passed them, going home to Agrippias after a long day of labor. Some made the sign against evil in the dusk as they hurried by.

Zarathan didn't know what to make of it. "Why do they do that?"

"They are simple, uneducated people, Zarathan. Perhaps they believe that three monks in filthy robes are apostates."

"Three monks in filthy robes, traveling with a woman," he said in a low voice. "That's our problem."

Barnabas didn't respond, but surely he knew that Kalay's presence didn't help matters. What would a decent woman be doing traveling with three monks in good standing? The more Zarathan thought about it, they did resemble a band of outcasts, even brigands. If he'd had the strength, he would have scowled at her, for all the good it would have done. She'd probably just give him another of her licentious winks, and then he'd be suffering in more than just his belly.

"It's chilly tonight." Barnabas shivered, and let out a shaky breath.

Zarathan frowned. It was a cool night, but not that cool. For days, they'd been sleeping out beneath the stars in just their thin robes. Had a chill settled in the old man's bones? It wouldn't be surprising. Every time he'd awakened in the past few days, he'd seen Cyrus standing guard and Barnabas kneeling in prayer. The only one who seemed to sleep truly well was Kalay, but then she had her long black cape to comfort her.

"Why did that man at the village call Libni 'Old Scary'?" Zarathan asked.

"Very holy people are always scary, Zarathan. The light of God shines from their eyes like fiery pokers. Ordinary people find it unsettling," Barnabas replied, looking at the empty ocean. The water stretched westward, flowing to the edges of the earth, and the monsters that inhabited the eternal depths.

"I've always thought hermits were an odd lot," Zarathan said. "I can't imagine living most or all of my life without other people close by. What's Libni like?"

Barnabas turned and, in the blue-gray darkness, Zarathan saw the old monk's gray brows pull down. He stared at the seagulls for a long time, before he whispered, "When I knew him, he was a laughing youth, always tripping over his own feet, but very studious and devoted to the words of our Lord. Of course, that was before the murder of his wife."

"His wife was murdered?"

Zarathan's voice had risen and attracted Cyrus's attention. He slowed his horse to ride alongside them. "Whose wife was murdered?"

"Libni's," Barnabas said. "It was an ugly crime. He

3

was never the same after that. At least, that's what I heard. I left Caesarea right after it happened."

Kalay asked, "Did they ever catch the murderer?"

"Oh, yes. We found him. He'd fled to the church and was hiding there."

They rode past a wave-smoothed boulder and out onto a plain of glimmering seashells that crunched beneath their horses' hooves. Far ahead, a wall of starlit cliffs glowed.

Fascinated, Zarathan said, "What did you do?"

"I and the other library assistants surrounded the church. We whispered our prayers into the stones, begging God to reveal him to us. Then we fashioned talismans with the sign of the dove and the lamb and carried them before us into the dark nave. He laughed at us, threw things. We captured him in the bell tower. From there, he was dragged to his death."

"You killed him?" Zarathan blurted, astonished. "You killed a man?"

"No, I didn't," Barnabas said softly. "Libni did. He dragged him out of the church and beat him to death with his bare hands. Though we tried, there was nothing we could do to stop him."

Zarathan exchanged a grave look with Cyrus, but before either of them could speak, Kalay commented with her usual aplomb. "My kind of man. I like him already."

Zarathan looked at her as if she were a half-wit, but the she-demon didn't seem to notice.

A breath of wind blew in off the ocean, whispered across the sand at the level of the horses' hooves, and brought the watery scents of fish and seaweed.

4

"Brothers, do you see that?" Cyrus asked and pointed. "There. Is that the pillar?"

Zarathan leaned sideways to peer around Barnabas. Standing between two humps of rock, the pillar resembled a finger lifted in warning.

"I've seen that before," Kalay mused. "Men usually greet me that way."

Zarathan cringed in shocked humiliation. "You are so vile! They're just rocks!"

She nonchalantly lifted a shoulder. "Rocks are rocks."

Barnabas called, "Look! Perhaps those are Libni's caves!"

As they rode closer to the black holes that pocked the cliffs, Zarathan kept shooting disgruntled glances at Kalay, but she was ignoring him. It was infuriating.

Cyrus said, "There must be hundreds of them. How will we find Libni's?"

"We'll search every one, if necessary."

"But that could take forever, and we're almost certainly being followed. If we don't find him quickly, shouldn't we just move on?" When Barnabas didn't answer, Zarathan turned to Cyrus. "Brother, surely you see the wisdom of losing ourselves in a city where it's more difficult to track us?"

Cyrus was examining the rimrock and the tumbled boulders that clustered at the base of the cliffs. Without so much as glancing at Zarathan, he said, "We can hide in a cave as easily as a city. If, as Barnabas believes, Libni can help us understand the papyrus, it's worth the risk."

"Zarathan, our brothers died because of it," Barnabas said with reverence. "We owe it to them to find out why."

As they rode closer to the cliff, a tiny thread of light glinted in one of the caves, then vanished as though it had never been.

Cyrus said, "Did you—"

"I saw it," Barnabas answered and kicked the horse into a shambling trot. "Let's find out."

2

A young man, perhaps sixteen, met them at the cave entrance. He was short and ugly, with black, vulnerable eyes. His head had been shaved, probably in penance for some affront. As he stepped toward them, the coarse fabric of his brown robe molded to each hard muscle.

He said, "I am Tiras, assistant to the blessed hermit. How may I help you?"

Barnabas carefully took hold of his book bag, dismounted, and handed the reins to Zarathan. A tattered curtain covered the cave entrance. Through the rips, warm golden light streamed. "I am Brother Barnabas, here to see my old friend Libni, if this is where he lives."

The youth's eyes flew wide. "Oh! He said you were coming!" He swiftly ducked beneath the curtain and a golden glow of firelight flashed across the sand. Soft voices rose inside.

Barnabas turned to the others and said, "You may dismount. All is well."

"Really?" Kalay said suspiciously. "How did he know you were coming?"

"Libni probably foresaw it. He's always had visions."

In the early days, Barnabas had been jealous, wondering why God had chosen to reveal himself to Libni and not to him. Barnabas had studied harder, prayed harder, and worked harder. But over the decade they'd been together, his jealousy had mutated into deep reverence. Libni *had* been chosen, and he was grateful to know a man favored by God.

"That's not a very good answer, brother." Kalay's mouth quirked. "Especially not after what we heard in the last village. Someone else was looking for Libni. I'd say it's likely the sicarii got here before we did and are waiting to greet us."

Barnabas turned in irritation. "Kalay, if that were the case, don't you think Libni would have ordered his assistants to warn us?"

"Not if a dagger is poised over Libni's heart."

"You have so little faith. Please, trust me. All is well. You may dismount." He clutched his bag to his chest.

Despite her misgivings, Kalay dismounted, followed by Zarathan, leaving Cyrus alone on his horse.

"Cyrus," Barnabas said. "Come, join us."

His horse tossed its head, and the reins clinked. "I need to scout the area. I'll leave as soon as I know that you are safe here."

"Very well." Barnabas sighed, realizing that arguing would be fruitless. "I'll send Kalay back as soon as we've met Libni."

"Good."

Tiras ducked beneath the door curtain again, followed by another young man, perhaps thirteen, with wavy red hair, green eyes, and freckles. Clearly of Celtic descent.

Tiras said, "My master bids you enter," and thrust out a hand to the entrance.

Barnabas shoved aside the curtain and ducked inside. Tiras and the other youth followed him.

The interior, lit by distant candlelight, was much larger than he'd suspected. The roof of this particular cave rose twenty cubits over his head, but there were tunnels going off in every direction from this main chamber. The faint warmth penetrated his thin robe and made Barnabas shiver in relief.

Zarathan and Kalay entered and stood behind him.

Kalay adjusted her weapons belt and asked, "Where's the murderer? Out on a jaunt?"

Tiras frowned at her as though mystified by the comment, but vaguely aware that he ought to be insulted by it.

Barnabas turned. "I've seen no one since I entered. Perhaps he's in another chamber."

He took two steps forward, but Tiras said, "No, not that way, brother. Please, follow me." He held out a hand to the tunnel on the right, showing them the way.

As Barnabas and Kalay followed the two young monks into the dark tunnel, Zarathan called shrilly, "I'll stay here to keep watch!"

Kalay turned and acidly said, "Cyrus will feel so much better with you at his back."

At the end of the passageway was a large, smoky chamber. The candles on the long table cast a flickering

9

gleam over the stone wall. Over thirty cubits across, the rounded chamber rose another ten cubits over their heads. Holes of every size and shape honeycombed the walls, and each was stuffed with books, scrolls, writing instruments, and ink.

Barnabas smiled. Even in the middle of the desert, a librarian could not survive without books. He set his precious book bag on the table and turned to Kalay. "Please go and tell Cyrus that all is well."

Kalay's thin red brows lifted. "You're a gullible soul, Barnabas. I've seen nothing to suggest safety, let alone—"

The curtain on the far side of the chamber was thrown back and Libni—older, more grizzled—rushed into the chamber in a whirl of threadbare brown rags that fluttered around him like an ancient shroud.

"Tiras! Uzziah! Fetch us down some wine and food," Libni ordered, passing between the startled youths. Libni almost flew across the floor and embraced Barnabas in a bear hug that nearly cracked his ribs. "Barnabas, my dear old friend! How good of you to come see me! It's been what, twenty years? Twenty-one? Did you ever find the village of Asthemo?"

He was a massive man, tall, with the meaty shoulders of an ox, and hands twice the size of Barnabas's. A loose mane of graying brown hair framed his bearded face.

Barnabas pulled away from his strong arms and laughed. "Not yet. I'm still looking."

"I always thought it was in the region of Eleutheropolis."

"As I do. I just haven't found any evidence to

support that suspicion." He held out a hand to Kalay, and introduced her. "Libni, this is my friend Kalay."

At some point in the past twenty heartbeats, Kalay had drawn her knife and fallen into a she-wolf's crouch.

Libni turned and went still, looking at her with wide gray eyes. In a tender voice, he said, "At first I thought you were an angel. Now I am genuinely delighted to discover you are flesh and blood. Please, both of you, be seated. My brothers will arrive shortly with refreshments."

Kalay nonchalantly kept her knife at the ready. "I'll stand."

"But you must be tired, please sit."

"No."

Libni frowned. "You're going to stand all night after you've been riding hard for days?"

"Possibly."

Libni's mad eyes flared a little wider. "You don't say much, do you?"

Kalay tilted her head. "Well, if you leave out all the pig shit in life, you don't need many words."

A slow smile came to Libni's lips, and he let out a belly laugh that boomed from the cave walls. "A beautiful woman with a sense of humor! I've been blessed by God."

Kalay squinted at him, straightened, and shoved her dagger into its sheath. "You've a curious way of looking at things, brother."

"Yes, but don't let that worry you. I'm harmless."

Under her breath, she said, "That's not what I've heard."

Then louder, added, "Forgive me, but I must go tell my companions that it's safe."

"Well, of course, it's safe," Libni said, a bit indignantly.

Kalay gave him an incredulous glance and left.

Libni watched her duck into the tunnel, and affection melted his face. "Her eyes remind me of Sousanna's. Do you remember how blue they were? Like pieces of the sky fallen to earth."

"I do remember. I think it is Kalay's misfortune that she reminds every man of a woman he's lost."

A pained smile turned Libni's lips. "Yes," he replied softly, "I can see how that might lead a girl's soul astray. How does she come to be in your company?"

"She was the washerwoman at the monastery."

Libni arched an eyebrow. "What did you do to make our Lord so eager to test the chastity of your monks?"

Barnabas suppressed a smile. "Nothing I'm aware of."

Libni thoughtfully smoothed a hand over his unkempt beard. "And before she was a washerwoman? What did she do?"

"I don't know how she earned her way in life. None of that matters to me."

A sad reverie filled Libni's eyes. "Has she repented?"

"No, and I wouldn't bring it up if I were you. I overheard her say that most of her family was killed during the Persecution. She blames the Church." Barnabas remembered the conversation he'd inadvertently overheard between Cyrus and Kalay that morning on the shore of the Nile. He had wondered then if he shouldn't speak with her, but had decided to wait.

"That is unfortunate. When the time is right, I'm sure you will discuss our Lord's teachings with her."

"I'll ponder the risk of a dagger between my ribs if we survive our current dilemma."

Libni gestured to the dark high-backed chairs around the table. "Sit. Tell me what brings you here."

Barnabas eased into one of the chairs and exhaled hard. "You're looking better than I would have thought."

Libni seated himself at the end of the table. As he leaned forward to brace his elbows on the dark wood, his shoulder-length hair fell forward. His sparkling eyes were half insane and filled with tears. "I dreamed you were coming. God told me to prepare for your arrival. I am so glad to see you."

"God told you?" Awe filled Barnabas, just like in the old days.

"Oh, yes." Libni looked around the cave. "Every stone here breathes the Word of God. What He did not tell me is why you were coming."

Barnabas leaned across the table to touch Libni's hand. For several moments, they just stared at each other. "I need your help."

"With what? Something in that old gazelle leather bag?" He gestured to the book bag resting on the far end of the table.

"Partly. We are on a mission of great importance." He lowered his voice to a whisper. "Do you remember the papyrus?"

Libni's smile faded. Despite the fact that they had translated hundreds of scrolls, codices, and fragments of papyri in their lives, there was only one that deserved a whisper. Libni took Barnabas's hand in both of his and crushed his fingers. "You found it! Tell me you *found* it!"

"No, no, I'm sorry to get your hopes up. That's why I'm here."

Disappointment slackened Libni's features, and his gray eyes flared as though in sudden understanding. "You're in danger, aren't you? Because of the papyrus?"

"More danger than I can tell you. Some days ago, a bishop from Rome came to our monastery to deliver the edicts of the Council of Nicea. That night, the monastery was attacked. The supper was poisoned. Everyone was killed, murdered because of the books. Two brothers and I—and Kalay—escaped down the Nile in her boat. I'm certain we're still being followed."

"By whom?"

Barnabas shook his head. "The name of the bishop from Rome was Meridias. Libni, if they're terrified enough to kill dozens of innocent monks, they'll do anything. After we leave, you should take precautions."

Libni cocked his head and gave Barnabas a singularly gentle smile. "I've been trying to die for more than twenty years, my friend, and God has not allowed it. I will, however, take precautions. Not for myself, but for the young men who have chosen to study with me."

"I was surprised to see the youths here. I thought you were a hermit?"

"I was." Libni shrugged helplessly. "Now I'm a teacher."

It must have been many years since anyone had visited Libni, let alone come to "study" with him, and the fact seemed to bring him great joy.

He said, "I truly appreciate the lengthy conversations and even more lengthy scriptural readings my

14

brothers and I share. I had forgotten the serenity of a spiritual community."

Uzziah and Tiras returned, carrying two plates heaped with bread, cheese, and jugs of wine surrounded by chipped ceramic cups. As they set them on the table between Barnabas and Libni, Tiras said, "Brother Barnabas, your companions are on their way. Is there anything else I might bring you?"

"No, Tiras. Thank you very much."

Kalay and Zarathan emerged from the tunnel, and Zarathan's nose started to wiggle. He almost ran across the room to plop himself down in the chair closest to the plates of food. Fortunately, he did not grab for anything, but peered at the feast like a predator about to pounce.

Libni said, *"Kairos,"* and bowed his head.

Barnabas and Zarathan joined him in praying. "Glory be to the Father and to the Son and to the Holy Spirit, as it was in the beginning, is now, and ever shall be, world without end. Amayne."

When he lifted his head, Barnabas found Kalay staring at him with a distasteful squint to her eyes.

Libni said, "Here, allow me to pour the wine while you help yourselves to the bread and cheese."

Zarathan's hand moved faster than a serpent striking. He had a slice of cheese in his mouth before Libni had even fully risen to his feet, and with his other hand was in the process of snatching a chunk of bread.

Kalay, sounding a little bored, said, "I think you missed your calling, Zarathan. You should have been a pickpocket."

Around a mouthful of food, Zarathan slurred something unpleasant that sounded vaguely like "You ought to know."

Libni poured four cups of wine and handed them around the table before he seated himself again, and noted, "I think that was an attempt to asperse your character, my dear."

"Oh, yes, sitting over there all the way across the table, he's very brave. Unlike me. I won't insult someone unless they're close enough to knife."

That silenced the chamber. Every man stared at her as she nonchalantly ripped off a piece of bread, ate it, and washed it down with a long drink of wine.

Once she'd swallowed, she said, "I hope Brother Barnabas told you that we're being followed by crazed killers, and you might want to boot us out at first chance."

"Yes. He told me." Libni nodded. "But who are these men? Surely, you have some notion?"

Barnabas began, "They may be—"

Kalay interrupted, "Oh, they're devout men—probably spend their lives with their knees stuck to a floor—but they're well-trained in the military arts. Likely they're members of some secret organization mustered to protect the mysteries of your faith."

Surprised, Libni said, "Which organization?"

"I suspect—" Barnabas tried.

Kalay interrupted again. "My guess is they're Militia Templi. But they might be—"

"Kalay, would you mind if I answer some of Libni's questions?" Barnabas scowled at her.

"Not a bit, brother." She extended a hand, telling him to go on. "Assuming you don't mince words in an effort to protect your holy brethren."

Barnabas sighed in irritation. "The one thing we know for certain is that they came from Rome with orders to burn all the documents recently declared heretical, and to kill anyone who's ever read them."

Libni stared down into his cup, watching the candlelight reflect from the rich red liquid. "Strange."

"What is?" Zarathan took another bite of cheese. "That they came to burn the documents? Or kill anyone who'd read them?"

"Well, I should think both. But that would suggest that they..."

His voice faded, and Barnabas frowned. "That would suggest that they what?"

"Hmm?" Libni gazed at him as though he had no idea what he was talking about.

"You said that the fact that they would burn the documents, and kill anyone who'd read them, would suggest something...what?"

A breath of wind penetrated the cave and the flickering candles cast odd shadows over Libni's intent face. In a voice just above a whisper, he said, "Did you know that I once killed a man?"

Kalay and Zarathan both stopped eating and were regarding Libni with wide eyes. His devoted students, Uzziah and Tiras, appeared frozen with shock.

"Libni," Barnabas said soothingly. His old friend's tormented expression broke his heart. "I was there. Of course, I know."

Libni wet his lips. "Were you?"

"Yes, my friend. Don't you remember? We sat for the longest time staring at the stars, talking about forgiveness."

Tears drained down Libni's cheeks. "Oh, yes. Yes, now I recall." He smiled his love at Barnabas. "How could I have forgotten? You helped me that terrible night."

Barnabas reached out to put his fingers on Libni's threadbare sleeve. "God forgave you long ago, my friend. You don't need to keep punishing yourself for it. Let it go."

As though he'd suddenly come back, Libni pulled himself up straight in his chair. "Since that day, I have believed that murder is grief taken to the extreme. It is a desperate act of bereavement. If these truly are Church-sanctioned killers, then what is the source of the bereavement? What loss does our Church fear so much it would resort to murder?"

In a hoarse whisper, Barnabas said, "Have you heard about the declarations of the Nicean synod?"

"We get very little news out here. What declarations?"

"Libni, a synod of bishops just met in Nicea. They cast out the gospels of Maryam, Philippon, Thomas, and many other books, even the Shepherd of Hermas."

"But that's *absurd!*" Libni exploded, half rising out of his chair. Just as suddenly he went absolutely quiet, and a foreboding stillness filled the cave, broken only by the spluttering of the candles. As he sank back down to his seat, he murmured, "Oh. Of course."

Zarathan glanced around at each person in the room before he asked, "Why?"

Libni stared straight at Barnabas. "It's the fleshly resurrection and the virgin birth, isn't it?"

Barnabas replied, "They just decreed both to be fact and apparently consider them to be the two doctrines that will bind Christianity together."

Libni's mouth quivered. "You mean they think they

need a few miracles for the masses, or they won't believe our Lord's teachings?"

"I think so."

Libni squeezed his eyes closed.

Uzziah and Tiras looked stunned that two old monks would dare to speak such heresy aloud. As they had during their time together in Caesarea, Libni probably said the Creed four times a day and instructed his brothers to do the same. The youths had to be completely confused by their discussion.

Libni opened his eyes and gazed steadily at the dark tabletop. "They have cast aside our Lord's own words." In a very small voice, he recited, "Truth is a life-eater."[1]

"They fear the Truth more than anything." After several taut heartbeats, Barnabas continued, "That's why they want to destroy the papyrus and anyone who has ever read it."

Candlelight glinted in Libni's eyes as his gaze bored into Barnabas's. "If the fools think we understand it, they obviously give us more credit than we are due."

"We must try harder. Before it's too late."

Libni took a long drink of his wine, set his empty cup down with a thud, and in a forlorn voice asked, "Do you really think they would destroy the Pearl?"

"They must. You know it as well as I do."

Kalay sat forward. "You mean you know what the Pearl is?"

Barnabas remained mute, staring at Libni.

Libni's gaze drifted over the arching stone ceiling and moved silently from one overstuffed hole in the wall to the next. Finally, he grunted softly and rose to his feet, answering, "Well, let's say we have a good guess."

"A guess? Killers are hunting you down over a 'guess'?"

Barnabas ran a hand through his dirty gray hair and sighed. "They don't realize all we have is a guess, Kalay. I'm sure they think we know everything."

In an innocent voice, Kalay said, "Well, then, why don't you just tell them you don't know anything? Maybe they'll stop trying to kill you. Did you ever think of that?"

Barnabas gave her an annoyed look. "We don't want them to know we're as ignorant as we are. The more time we have, the more likely we are to decipher the papyrus."

She gruffly folded her arms. "You two have bishop potential."

Libni walked to a stash of scrolls. As though touching a frail and beloved child, he lifted one and brought it back to the table.

He rested his hand protectively on top of it as he spoke. "There is a passage I've been meaning to write you about."

Barnabas could tell from the grave tone of his voice that it might refer to the papyrus. In a subtle gesture, he tipped his head toward Tiras and Uzziah. "What do you think?"

Libni studied his students with moist eyes. "Tiras? Why don't you take Uzziah and lay out blankets for our guests. After that, please retire to the reading cave and study the Acts of John. Pay particular attention to the passages regarding our Lord's suffering. We will discuss them tomorrow."

"Yes, Abba Libni," Tiras said and turned to the table. "Peace be with you, brothers and sister."

"And peace be with you, Tiras and Uzziah," Barnabas responded. Between chews, Zarathan echoed his words. Kalay gave them a disturbing smile.

Both youths looked startled, and left.

Barnabas and Libni next turned and peered at Kalay. She understood immediately and pursed her lips as though she'd just eaten something sour. "Well enough. I didn't want to hear your prattle anyway. I'll go and wait for Brother Cyrus to return."

She rose and strode into the tunnel that led outside.

Barnabas looked back at Libni, who softly added, "I think perhaps we should talk alone, just the two of us."

Zarathan, who had a mouthful of bread, choked it down. "But I know all about the papyrus! I helped translate some of the words."

Barnabas nodded obligingly. "Yes, you did, and I was grateful; but Libni and I have many things to discuss. The papyrus is only one of them. Perhaps it would be better if you waited outside with Kalay. That way, when Cyrus returns, you can lead him here to this chamber and we'll all discuss the papyrus together."

"Kalay could do that just as well as me." Zarathan angrily shoved back his chair, grabbed another chunk of bread, and stalked from the room.

Libni watched the retreat with kind eyes. "Pride is his greatest obstacle."

"As I've told him many times."

"How long has he been a monk?"

"Three months."

Barnabas lifted his cup and took a sip of wine. He could feel Libni's eyes upon him, heavy with the weight of their next words.

Libni waited until the voices in the outer cave had

faded before he whispered, "How many of the Occultum Lapidem are left?"

"The two of us, and I pray that Symeon is still alive in Apollonia."

Libni petted the scroll that lay upon the table. "Barnabas, I believe I may have found the answer in the Gospel of Nikodemos."

"Nikodemos? But I've read it a thousand times. Where? What verses?"

"The story of Yosef Haramati." He used the man's Hebrew name, rather than the more familiar Greek, Ioses of Arimathaia. "Do you remember? After he placed our Lord's body in his garden tomb, Annas and Kaiaphas were enraged. They ordered him arrested. While they discussed his fate, they imprisoned Yosef for a week in a room without a window."

"A room with one door, to which Kaiaphas had the only key."[2]

"Yes." Libni's voice was a hiss in the stillness.

For a few brief moments, Barnabas could hear the ocean. Waves crashed upon the shore, and he wondered if a storm had arisen.

"What else, Libni?"

"When Kaiaphas unlocked the door on the first day of the week, the room was empty. Yosef was gone."

"Yes, yes. I know all that. What does the story have to do with—"

"Don't you see? The priests went searching for Yosef after Phinees, Adas, and Angaeus came from the Galilaian to Jerusalem, and told the high priests, 'We saw Yeshua and his disciples sitting upon the mountain of Mamlich.' They thought he was alive! They said, 'Give us Yosef Haramati and he will give you Yeshua.'

They truly believed that Yosef knew where our Lord was and would betray him. But they found Yosef's prison empty!"

Libni's face was alight. He was relating the story as though it had just happened days ago, rather than centuries.

Patiently, Barnabas inquired, "What does that have to do with the papyrus?"

Libni leaned forward until his nose was less than a cubit from Barnabas's face. In a wine-scented whisper, he said, "Yosef had spent that entire week on the run, he—"

"Libni, I've read the Gospel of Nikodemos. Papias reports this same story, with a few variations, in his *Logia*. What does it have to do with the papyrus?"

"Oh, Barnabas," he said with true amusement and joy. "You're going to be so surprised when I tell you—"

Voices rose in the next chamber, followed by footsteps in the tunnel. Kalay ducked into the chamber, then Zarathan and Cyrus followed.

The wind must have picked up, for Cyrus's black curly hair had been blown back from his bearded face, making his straight nose seem longer, his eyes more like hard, shimmering emeralds.

"Cyrus," Barnabas introduced, "this is my friend Libni. He is a great scholar of the ancient texts."

Cyrus came around the table and bowed to Libni. His once white robe, torn and streaked with dirt, old blood, and soot, clung to his tall body. "Brother, thank you for sheltering us tonight. I promise we will be gone before dawn."

Libni placed a gentle hand on Cyrus's bowed head. "You must sit and eat to restore your strength for the long journey ahead. Please, let me pour you some wine."

Cyrus cast a glance at Barnabas, as though he could shed light on the "long journey" comment.

Barnabas merely said, "Sit down, Cyrus. I'll explain soon. What did you find outside?"

Cyrus took a chair and reached for the loaf. As he tore off a chunk, he said, "I scouted the area. While I saw no one, there are tracks everywhere. I could make no sense of them, which means I have no idea if we are safe or not."

Libni spilled some wine on the table beside Cyrus's cup and, as he wiped it up with his sleeve, said, "Of course there are tracks everywhere. The coastline is a major thoroughfare. Fishermen, traders, merchants, even whole caravans move up and down the length of it."

Libni finished filling every cup on the table, including his own, and eased back down to his chair. When he looked again at Barnabas, his gray eyes had a curious glitter.

Barnabas, exasperated, said, "Libni, just quickly give me a clue. Then we'll open the discussion to everyone else."

Libni sat back in his chair. "Do you know what *mahanayim* means?"

Every gaze fixed on Libni.

Annoyed at the game, Barnabas said, "There are many possibilities. What do you think it means?"

Libni smiled his love at Barnabas, which defused some of his frustration. "I think it means 'two camps.'"

"Two camps?"

"Yes. It's so simple, isn't it? It's hard to believe we missed it all these years."

There were three or four heartbeats of incomprehension in the room, before Kalay gasped, "Blessed Mother! And 'Mehebel' means 'from the coast'!"

A tingling rush of heat flushed Barnabas's veins. "'Two camps from the coast.'" His hand shook as he reached out to touch Libni's wrist. "Dear God, then it *is* a map."

3

K alay sat in the high-backed chair with her knees drawn up, sipping wine while she watched the two old men who stood leaning over the ancient maps on the table. Brittle and yellowed, dotted here and there with drips of candle wax, Libni would allow no one but himself and Barnabas to touch the maps. The four other men had to stand back, watching from one or two paces away as their elders pondered the meaning of the faint, archaic symbols.

"That's the problem," Libni murmured, frowning. "We don't know where to start. There were eight major cities on the coast at the time of our Lord. Which one is the papyrus referring to?"

Candlelight lay like a thick amber resin on the surface of the tabletop. It seemed to catch in glowing lines on the edges of the maps.

"If the beginning point is a city at all," Cyrus countered as he paced behind Libni and Barnabas, his arms folded across his broad chest. "It could be a cove, a standing stone, a ruin, anything. There's no way to know."

Barnabas placed a hand on one curled map corner, carefully flattening it out so that he could read it. "If we are correct that the man who wrote the papyrus was Ioses of Arimathaia, then perhaps we should look at sites closest to Jerusalem."

"Why?" Cyrus asked skeptically.

"No reason really, except that's where he lived, and it gives us a starting place."

Libni's finger was moving through the air above the parchment. "The choices, in that case, would be Apollonia, Ioppe, and Ashkelon. Pick one."

Barnabas waved a hand uncertainly. "The one in the middle."

"Ioppe, or do you say *Yapo?*"

"Ioppe."

They both leaned over the table, staring at the map like scavenger birds waiting for their prey to die.

Kalay sighed. Though she had traveled much of Palestine and Egypt, she did not believe she had seen any place as desolate as the honeycomb of caves that Libni and his students called home. The chambers were virtually empty, except for a blanket folded in the corner where someone slept, or a prayer rug and a candle sitting in the middle of a swept dirt floor. Elsewhere in the region, people might live in caves, but the chambers had color. The walls were painted or contained colorful objects and bright fabrics, beads, or polished stones. Except for the library where she sat, this place was barren, the walls hollowed and smoothed by eons of wind and water. There was little here to break the monotony. Fortunately, the wine was tasty. She took another drink.

The faint creak of Cyrus's sword belt broke the silence as he shifted to prop one hand on the hilt. "How many stadia is it from Ioppe to Jerusalem?"

Libni rubbed his bearded chin. "Perhaps three hundred fifty or a little more. Why?"

"Because that means Jerusalem is 'two camps from the coast.'"

"Not if you're traveling on foot, it's at least three camps."

Cyrus lifted his chin, and Kalay could see the thoughts flashing behind his eyes. "If Ioses of Arimathaia is the writer, he was a powerful and renowned leader of the Temple. He must have had friends all over Palestine, people who would have helped him. I suspect he was on horseback."

Libni and Barnabas looked at each other, as though to see what the other thought. Finally Barnabas said, "Let's assume he's right."

"I agree. Does that mean then that Jerusalem is the place that is 'two camps from the coast'?"

"That's circular logic. That's where we started from." Barnabas grimaced. "If we assume that Ioppe is the starting place, it is just as likely that Mount Gerizim is the place 'two camps from the coast.'"

Kalay hugged her knees to her chest and said, "Well, if those are the choices, I'm of a mind to agree with Cyrus."

Zarathan scowled at her as though upset she'd spoken. He looked from man to man, clearly waiting for someone to reprimand her.

"Go on," Libni said. "Why?"

"Because the next word is *mahray*. David's champion was from the hill country of Judah, southwest of Bet Lehem, which is close to Jerusalem."

Libni's bushy gray brows lifted in admiration. "And what of *manahat*?"

She sat up straight and lowered her bare feet to the cold floor. "Well, if I'm following you, and going for a literal translation, I'd say it means 'resting place.'"

A warm, half-demented grin brightened Libni's face. "You are such a surprise. Where did you learn Hebrew?"

"My grandmother was Jewish. She read me the scriptures in Hebrew every night."

Libni's smile widened. "Then you should know what *magdi*—"

Zarathan piped up, "Magdiel was an Edomite chief." He was obviously pleased with himself for remembering. An arrogant smile tugged at the corners of his lips.

Libni said, "Yes, but not in this case."

Zarathan's smile drooped. "What do you mean? We all agreed that it was an Edomite chief!"

Libni's fond gaze fixed on Kalay. "Do you know, my dear?"

"I know that the translation of the word is God's gift, or the gift of God."

Cyrus's eyes widened. He propped his hand on the table and murmured, "Two camps from the coast... David's champion...lay to rest?...God's gift?"

Barnabas's knees seemed to go weak. He gingerly lowered himself to a chair and said, "God's gift, God."

"What does that mean?" Zarathan's mouth puckered into a pout. "It's gibberish."

Wind whipped around the chamber, fluttering the maps on the table, and Libni carefully reached out to hold down the corners.

Ignoring Zarathan, Kalay said, "After that, we've a problem."

"Because *selah* breaks the pattern," Zarathan said a little too loudly and thrust out his blond-fuzzed chin.

It truly amazed Kalay that he *had* been listening. She'd thought his head filled with nothing but bawdy paintings.

"Yes, it does," Libni agreed, and the wrinkles in his forehead deepened. "You have all clearly been considering this. What conclusions did you come to regarding *selah*?"

Barnabas braced his elbows on the table and answered, "We thought it might refer to the Edomite rock city, or perhaps the place in Moab."

"But," Kalay pointed out, "it literally means 'rock.'"

The men shifted, apparently waiting for someone to say something.

"God's gift, God, rock?" Zarathan asked, as though annoyed. "That's ridiculous."

"Maybe not." When Cyrus began pacing again, the flickering candlelight gilded his sword with a heartbeat of fire. "Is it possible that *Selah* could be a hidden reference to Saint Petros? His name also means 'rock.'"

"Yes, but in Hebrew 'rock' is *kepha*," Kalay said.

Libni steepled his fingers and propped his chin upon the point. "I hadn't thought of that one," he praised. "That's exactly the sort of twist Ioses of Arimathaia would throw in to confuse the idle reader. What do you think, Barnabas?"

Barnabas ran a hand through his gray hair. In the

muted light, his deeply sunken eyes turned glassy. "It is possible, but...it doesn't feel right."

"Well enough," Libni said, picked up the jug, and poured himself another cup of wine. "Let's move on to *massa, massa.* Cyrus? Your thoughts?"

"I thought it might be a reference to the son of Ishmael mentioned in the Book of Genesis."

Without being asked, Kalay offered, "I'm fairly sure it's from the *massa umeriba,* which literally means 'proof and strife,' or maybe 'testing and contention.'"

Barnabas said, "It could just as easily refer to the 'oracle' taught to King Lemuel. The problem is the papyrus is not written in Hebrew, it's written in Latin, which was surely designed to lead the reader on a merry chase, for, without the Hebraic letters, we've no idea how each, word might truly be translated."

"Yes. Quite correct," Libni said. "*Massa* as it appears in Latin may be an exact transliteration from the Hebrew, but in Hebrew the word may have been pronounced *massha,* or *massah,* each with a different meaning. Without seeing the context in which the words occur, we cannot pretend to know their exact meaning."

Since Kalay had never learned to read, such distinctions had little impact on her, but Zarathan looked truly perplexed.

His blond brows pinched. "Two camps from the coast, David's champion lay to rest God's gift, God, rock, proof, proof? It's nonsense."

"Perhaps if we could decipher *selah* it would all be perfectly clear." Barnabas sighed.

The stone floor was cold. Kalay drew her feet into the chair again and propped her cup of wine on her knees, wondering about *selah*. It was an Edomite fortress city conquered by Amaziah, King of Judah. Could it refer to a fortress made of stone? If the papyrus was, truly, a clever map, finding the fortress would be essential.

She leaned her head against the chair's back and let her gaze drift over the rounded candlelit ceiling. The men had lowered their voices, and begun talking softly among themselves.

Maybe Zarathan was right. It was all nonsense. She picked up the jug and refilled her cup again. A pleasant warmth was filtering through her veins, making all of this seem somehow less deadly than it was. She liked the few moments of respite.

In a nasty voice, Zarathan commented, "Soon, you're going to be slurring your words, then what will we do with you?"

She deliberately slurred, "I don't shink I want to answer that queshtion. It might give you ideas, and you've already got plenty in that young head of yoursh."

Red crept into his cheeks. He clamped his jaw and glowered at her. As though it would upset her, he announced, "I'm leaving. Where am I supposed to sleep?"

Libni looked up. "Tiras and Uzziah placed blankets in the entry cave for you, and they will be standing guard tonight so that you all can sleep without worry. Please try to rest."

Cyrus replied, "That will be a welcome relief. Thank you, brother."

Zarathan marched from the chamber, and Libni and Barnabas returned to the map. They whispered and pointed at different squiggly lines, lost in their own private conversation.

Cyrus gestured to Kalay to get her attention, then tilted his head toward the tunnel, silently asking her to join him outside.

Kalay rose to her feet and followed him.

In the entry cave, they found Zarathan rolled up in a blanket. Three other blankets lay folded in the rear. As they passed, Zarathan flopped to his opposite side, showing them his back, before they ducked outside.

Fog spun out of the sea, ghost white in the moonlight. Cyrus walked a few paces down the cliff face, taking them out of earshot of anyone who might be listening.

She walked along behind him, pondering why he needed to leave the caves to talk to her.

Finally, he stopped in a pool of cold shadows and leaned back against the cliff. Shreds of mist blew about him.

"What is your opinion of Libni?"

Kalay shrugged. "He's a curious one. I was unsure at first, but I like him."

"And his two assistants?"

"They're boys, Cyrus. They're no danger to us."

The world shimmered in the mist. His black hair and beard had already picked up an opalescent sheen.

"Do you believe Libni?" Cyrus cocked his head.

"If you're asking if I think the papyrus should be translated literally, it makes more sense than anything else we've tried."

"But Zarathan is right, it's gibberish."

"Everything is gibberish until you understand it, Cyrus."

She looked out at the oddly shaped boulders that thrust up from the surf. Moonlight streamed between them, bleaching the foamy water a stark silver color, and casting the rocks' inky shadows across the sand. As the fog floated over the dark sand toward them, she had the urge to try and summon the voices of the air and sea, as she'd been taught to do in the ancient mystery religion she followed. But she feared it might curdle Cyrus's Christian soul.

"What is 'God's gift'? Do you have any ideas?" he asked.

"Life. At least that's how I would answer that question. How would you?"

He gave her an uncertain half-shrug and shake of his head, but she could see the strange, somber expression on his handsome face.

"What's wrong, Cyrus?"

His gaze slid to her, but he paused for several moments before he said, "I think it's the Pearl."

"Which is...what?"

In the long silence that followed, Kalay heard one of their horses blow softly, and then the faint crunching of sand beneath hooves as the animals meandered along the beach, nipping every edible plant they could find. She kept her eyes on Cyrus. The lines at the corners of his eyes tightened. Finally, he answered, "You've heard us talk about Papias's book?"

"The *Lord's Logia?* Yes, what of it?"

While his gaze moved along the shoreline, he said, "The passage I read went something like this: 'The Son of Panthera will again put on his robe of glory, and call up the headless demon whom the winds obey when the Pearl is in hand.'"

"That's interesting. Or confusing."

"Yes," he said softly, "and that could be my fault, because I'm not skilled at Hebrew. I had to guess at many of the words." As though angry with himself, he slapped the grit from his sleeve.

They had taken refuge in the shadows of a tumbled pile of boulders that had cracked off the cliff sometime in the distant past and begun to sprout tiny wind-tortured trees. As the fog moved through, the branches sighed and shook water droplets onto the rocks. The blend of surf and dripping trees calmed her after the long days on the desert trail.

She braced her shoulder against the cliff and faced him. His gaze, however, was not on her, but on the fog, staring at it hard, as though trying to read their dire fortunes in the shifting patterns.

She asked, "What if the map leads nowhere and we're just chasing ghosts?"

"I believe in ghosts. Don't you?"

She hugged herself against the misty chill. "No."

"No? Really?" He sounded truly astounded. "What about angels and demons?"

"Ah." She waggled a finger at him. "I believe in demons, yes, I do. But I've seen them walking the streets, looked into their eyes, and seen evil looking back. Trust me, the world is filled with demons. Remember Loukas?"

He paused. "But no angels?"

"I've never seen one. Simple as that. When one appears, I'll reconsider."

In a deeply reverent voice, Cyrus said, "They exist, Kalay, believe me. They've saved me many times on the battlefield."

"I've seen you fight, Cyrus. I suspect it's a good deal more likely that you saved yourself. You're handy with a sword and dagger. Not only that, you're smart. You probably made the most of the few pieces of luck that turned your way." She shrugged. "But if you want to believe that angels whispered in your ears, that's your affair."

Cyrus smiled. She saw his teeth glint in the moonlight. "Perhaps that is a guardian angel's strength. There's never proof of his handiwork, which means that people must have faith."

"Faith that they're being watched over?" Her mouth tightened with disbelief. "Seems like a waste of effort to me."

"But you have faith," he pointed out. "You told me you're a goddess worshipper. Surely that requires as much faith as believing in angels."

She moved away from the cliff, straightened, and let her gaze roam the shadowed boulders. The mist had grown thicker, obscuring the gnarled trees, and she had a curious feeling that all was not as it seemed. She tried to shove the premonition away.

"The Goddess doesn't demand as much in return as your angels do," she replied. "My Goddess is happy with a prayer now and then, maybe a sacrifice on high holy days. She doesn't demand celibacy, or poverty, or any of the other unnatural things that your God does. The Goddess, as a result, is a whole lot easier to have faith in."

In a conspiratorial whisper, he said, "I think you're the most devout person I know. You just don't like to show it."

"And why would that be?"

"Because you're afraid it makes you look weak." He took a breath, and through a long exhalation said, "And weakness is something you of all people cannot afford."

Kalay considered him for several moments, watching the moonlight waver over his lips and flash in his eyes, surprised that he understood her so well. "Nor can you, I think. Though I suspect you believe your Lord would prefer it."

He shifted his back against the damp cliff, and fabric grated against stone. "There is not a night that passes that I don't feel Him seeking me in my dreams, calling to me to put away my sword and pick up His cross."

"Are you truly so deep a believer, Cyrus? I know you're a monk, but you don't seem to share their cowardly failings. At least, I haven't seen it."

"Haven't you?" His mouth curled into what could only be called a smile of self-loathing. "I'm afraid that what you see as my strengths I see as cowardice."

"Really? I'm surprised."

His gaze lowered, as though he didn't want to look at her when he said, "My Lord taught me to 'turn the other cheek,' to seek peace and love my neighbor. I believe those teachings with all my heart." His voice grew pained. "But I don't have the courage to follow them when people I care about have been murdered and others are in danger. But I should, Kalay, I should have the courage."

She opened her mouth to blurt something unpleasant, but his tormented expression stopped her. He had lifted his eyes and was gazing at her as though for reassurance. Perhaps he just wanted a few kind words?

Someone to tell him she believed in him and was grateful for all he'd done to protect them?

Instead, she said, "That's the problem with your Lord. He's always forcing people to give up everything they know, everything they are, and for what? Nothing."

He straightened at her hard tone. "I wouldn't call salvation 'nothing.' I'd much rather be saved than eternally damned."

"Is that what you fear? Damnation? Well, stop it. Your tradition teaches you that no matter what you do your Lord will forgive you, doesn't it?"

"No, there are certain sins that God cannot forgive, but—"

"I trust you're not planning on committing any of those, are you?"

He regarded her suspiciously. "No."

"Then what are you worried about? When all this is done, your Lord will forgive you your trespasses, and you can go back to following His teachings as though nothing happened."

He squinted at her. "You have a truly unbalanced way of looking at things."

She grinned. "That sounded like a backhanded compliment. Are you trying to be romantic?"

His mouth opened, but he couldn't seem to find the correct response.

"Good," she said, taking his arm. "Now that you're speechless, let's talk of more important things."

"What could possibly be more important than the salvation of my immortal soul?"

She guided him away from the boulders toward the

beach. "You told Libni we'd be gone before dawn. Where are we going?"

"I haven't the slightest idea. I assume that Libni and Barnabas will work out our route tonight."

"But we've only two choices, haven't we? Mount Gerizim or Jerusalem."

"Jerusalem," he said softly, as though feeling the names on his tongue. "It's so strange to call it that. For almost two hundred years it has been called by the name Emperor Hadrian gave it in the year 130: Aelia Capitolina. All my life, that's what I've called it."

"Well, Emperor Constantine just changed it back. It may be the one good thing he's done in his entire reign. Though Jews are still banned from entering the city, except on the ninth of the Hebrew month of Av."

"The ninth of Av? Why?"

She sucked in a breath, stunned by his ignorance. "That's the anniversary of the destruction of the Temple in the year 70. Jews are allowed to return to mourn the loss, and are tormented by Christians who circulate through the mourners berating them for continuing to weep and wait for the messiah. They shout that he's already come...that all the prophecies have been fulfilled, and Jews are just too stubborn to admit it."[1]

Cyrus's face tensed at the angry tone in her voice. "Have you visited Jerusalem on the ninth of Av?"

"My grandmother took me to the anniversary commemoration when I was five years old. I'll never forget how I felt. My parents were Christians, but I cannot tell you how very much I hated Christians that day."

Softly, Cyrus said, "I'm sorry."

Like most devout Christians, Cyrus believed Iesous was the messiah, and the destruction of the Temple was irrefutable proof that Iesous's prophecies had come true. It was enough to make her feel slightly ill.

She took a breath and let it out in a rush. "If we go there, we'll be riding into the lion's den, won't we?"

"Almost certainly. Bishop Macarios of Jerusalem is a close ally of Bishop Silvester's."

"Emperor Constantine's lackey?" she recalled. "Do you think he might be handing out daggers to our sicarii?"

"I think it's possible."

"Then I'd best get used to this fear that's been eating my belly for days."

As she released his arm and started to walk out onto the beach, he said, "Kalay?"

Even pitched low, his deep voice carried on the wind. She turned to find him gazing at her with pained eyes.

"Despite my beliefs, I will do everything I can to make certain we do not come to harm." He had his fists clenched at his sides, as though fighting the overwhelming urge to touch her.

"I've never doubted that, Cyrus."

"I know that you think I—" Cyrus went suddenly still and his gaze fastened on the sand at their feet. He cocked his head, as though listening.

After several moments of holding her breath, she whispered, "What is it?"

He pointed. The constant sea breezes had nearly covered them, but the dark spots of shadow that marred the sand could only be tracks.

She kneeled to examine them, trying to decide if

they'd been made by men or animals. "They're badly washed out, Cyrus."

She started to walk along them, and he reached out and took her hand with an unthinking intimacy. She flinched at his touch as though her soul were warning her to run.

"No, don't follow them," he ordered.

The warmth of his flesh against her cold fingers made her shiver. "Why not?"

"They're hoofprints."

"So? Libni told you, this coast is a thoroughfare. Fishermen, traders, merchants, even whole caravans move up and down the length of it."

"This was one man on a horse, riding very close to the surf, as close as he could."

"A scout hoping his tracks would be washed away quickly?"

"Maybe."

Looking across the sand, Kalay saw how the tracks curved with the line of the water, veering around a narrow spit of land, and disappearing into the unknown night beyond.

"Do you think it's one of our pursuers?" she asked.

Cyrus propped his hand on the hilt of his belted sword and his fingers tightened around the grip, as if ready to draw it against things unseen. "I always assume the worst. If it doesn't come about, I'm pleasantly surprised."

"You and I have learned the same lessons."

He turned to survey the white ribbon of foam that marked the waves. "I swear I—" He stopped and clamped his jaw.

A strange undercurrent filtered through the words.

She reached up and turned his face to look into his eyes. They were overflowing with guilt. He was holding something back, drowning in secrets that were eating him alive. "There's something you haven't told me, isn't there? Something you haven't told anyone. What is it?"

"I—I can't tell you."

She let her hand drop. "Is it about Loukas?"

He just stared at her. "You're too perceptive for your own good."

"I've been told that before. Best to tell me now, Cyrus."

He braced his feet. As though the words were being ripped from his chest by a hook, he croaked, "I—I remember where I've seen him."

"Where?"

"The day my wife died."

He turned to walk away, but Kalay grabbed his hand and jerked him back. Agony lined his face. As though he was expecting the question, his fingers crushed hers.

"When was that?"

He seemed to be struggling with himself, deciding which words to use.

"It was right after the Milvian Bridge battle. I—I just couldn't stand the hypocrisy." A hushed violence strained the words. "I deserted the army. The emperor sent men to bring me back—or maybe to kill me. They broke into my home in the middle of the night. I told Spes to run while I fought them off." His shoulders hunched and he seemed to fold in upon himself. "They killed her first."

"Right in front of you? You saw it?" His expression told her everything. She exhaled hard and nodded. For a brief moment, the mist parted and she saw the horses galloping along the beach in the moonlight, their manes and tails flying. Playful whinnies carried on the wind. "Was it Loukas who killed her?"

"No. He was the reason I got away."

"I don't understand."

He gripped his sword again, as though to comfort himself. "He was young. Inexperienced. I surprised and overpowered him, then ran. I doubt he ever completely lived down the humiliation. He was supposed to be guarding my door."

Kalay shivered and started back toward the caves. Cyrus walked behind her. Every so often she caught the jangle of the weapons on his belt, or heard his soft footsteps.

Just before they reached the entry cave, she turned. "Cyrus, what did you mean by 'the hypocrisy'? Not that I'm an admirer of Rome or the emperor, but you don't seem like the sort who would desert."

He stood perfectly still. The wind blew his curly black hair straight back, showing the smooth curves of his cheekbones and brow. "I was there that day."

"What day?"

"*The* day. The day before the battle."

She searched her memory, trying to figure out what he meant. "The day the emperor saw the cross in the sky?"

He snorted in disgust. "He'd been sitting in his tent all morning drinking wine. He called me in just after noon. I was his trusted adviser, and he needed my advice. He told me he had decided how to motivate our men to attack the bridge. The only part he couldn't decide was the exact form the myth should take."

"The myth?"

"Oh, yes. He was a master mythmaker. He knew exactly what he was doing. But he couldn't decide if he should see a cross of light or the letters *chi-rho*. You know, a kind of divine monogram? Or maybe he should simply hear angels singing 'By this conquer.'[2] He asked me which I liked better. I said I thought it was a foolish idea that would alienate many of our devoted Roman soldiers."

"And how did the emperor respond?"

"He threw me out of his tent."

The fog shifted, swirling around them in the glittering haze, and the shadows turned slippery and liquid.

"I think that's when it began to worry him."

"That you knew it was not a miraculous vision but a political ploy?"

"Yes."

Kalay folded her arms tightly over her chest. "I can't believe you're still alive."

"Nor can I."

"Have the Romans hunted you ever since?"

He rubbed his scabbard, as though smoothing away the drops of moisture that glistened on the leather. "I don't know."

She slowly lowered her arms. "I think that's the first lie you've told me."

He squeezed his eyes closed for a long moment, before saying, "They probably have. I do not know for certain, but I've often feared it."

Kalay put a hand on his broad shoulder. It was a friendly gesture, nothing more, but he uncertainly reached up, took her hand, and pulled her toward him.

His arms shook as he wrapped them around her. "Don't say anything. Just let me hold you for a few moments."

Stunned, she just stood there. A strange sensation of relief possessed her. Not desire, not love, just...relief. Which was totally foolish. They were being stalked by dedicated killers who might be watching them at this very instant. Though to see through this fog, they would have to be very close by.

Tenderly, she said, "I'm starting to hope you're right."

"About what?"

"About there being angels watching over us."

His grip relaxed slightly. He looked down at her. Something about the softness in his eyes touched her, building a warmth in her heart.

"Why?" he asked.

"Because both our guards are down. If I were a murderer, this is the moment I would strike."

He backed away and his gaze quickly searched the beach and the cliff. "You're right. Let's get back inside. If God is very good to us, tonight we'll get some sleep."

She let him walk past her, and followed a pace behind.

A half hour later, Kalay pulled the worn softness of the blanket up around her throat and stared at the dark ceiling high above. Cyrus and Zarathan were sound asleep. She'd been trying, but thoughts of Cyrus kept waking her. A sharp ache invaded her chest. She couldn't shake the sensation of his arms around her. It was as powerful as a polished golden calf in the searing deserts of old.

The Teaching on the Shadow

"Are you still there, brother?"

You roll over at his whisper and inhale a breath of the warm night air. Stars glisten overhead, and the breeze is redolent with the scents of damp earth and trees. He lies rolled in his blanket two cubits away with his head propped on his laced fingers, staring up at the darkness. Every time he blinks, his eyes catch the starlight and hold it for an instant.

"Of course I'm still here. Where else would I be?"

"I can't find you."

You prop yourself up on one elbow. "I'm right here. Turn and look at me."

You see his mouth curl in a smile. "I've been looking at you for months. I still can't find you."

Ah, now, you understand. He's being profound. You say, "Well, it's not my fault that you won't open your eyes. I'm so close to you that I could be your shadow, yet you are blind to me."

His smile fades as though it never existed. For several instants he does not speak. Finally, he says, "Shadows need light to live. They die in the darkness. I fear that's where you are, and why I can't find you."

You study his silhouette....he's the one who is the shadow tonight. The shadow of the darkness itself. "Yeshu, I am not in the dark. I am a shadow in love with the sun who hides out of self-preservation. That's why you can't find me."

He somberly turns to me. "What do you mean?"

"I mean I know what you're planning, and when the sun dies, all of the shadows it casts die just as completely. How can you be so heartless, so careless of those who love you?"

He takes a breath and exhales very slowly, as though cherishing the sensation of air moving in his lungs. "Are you afraid?"

You stare up at the stars again, at the way they silver the heavenly vault.

"Yes," you say. "I am afraid."

In a voice almost too soft to hear, he answers, "Then perhaps I have finally found you."

In the depths of the night, when only one candle continued to burn in Libni's library, Barnabas gently shoved the map aside and reached for a slice of goat cheese. As he took a bite, the rich flavor filled his mouth. They had been tossing ideas back and forth since he'd arrived, just as they used to at the library in Caesarea. Both of them were happy.

Libni broke off a piece of bread and, as he ate, his gaze filled with faraway places, memories that Barnabas could only guess at. After a long while, he reverently touched the corner of the papyrus. "Have you ever figured out why there is a large cross at the bottom of the papyrus, surrounded by three small crosses?"

"I'm not sure they are crosses."

"The central feature is a cross. It just has other symbols attached to it."

"Which means it may not be a Christian symbol at all. And if it is, it was almost certainly added decades later, probably by some pious monk. Not only that, the small crosses were definitely written in a different ink."

48

Prior to Constantine's vision, the cross had been viewed as the instrument of Iesous's execution, of his shame. As Saint Paul noted, it was a huge "stumbling block" to conversion.

The cross was not revered in and of itself, nor were Iesous and the cross seen as identical. One did not signify the other. There were many symbols revered by early Christians: the palm branch, the olive branch, the dove and the lamb, the anchor, the baptismal waters, the blood of Christ, the fish, or *ichthys*—because it was an acrostic of Iesous Christos, Son of God, Savior. But not the cross.

Then, thirteen years ago, Constantine's vision had changed all that. The cross had become the black blossom of the Church's imagination. It was painted on armor, shields, military standards, weapons of every variety, even gallows and prisons. It had become a symbol that Barnabas strongly suspected the savior himself would have abhorred. To Iesous and his disciples, the cross had not represented salvation, but absolute injustice and humiliation.

"I think you're right on both counts," Libni agreed. "It is not a Christian cross, and it was added by a very pious man: Ioses of Arimathaia, a devout Jew. The cross does not symbolize the crucifixion; it symbolizes something else. As do the small crosses."

Barnabas took another bite of the exquisitely aromatic cheese. "It sounds like you have an idea what that might be?"

Libni's mouth curled into a faint smile. He reached out, gripped the corner of the oldest, most frail map, and carefully dragged it across the table. His movements made the candle sputter. He positioned the map between them, then lifted and let his finger hover over a specific area. "Do you recall what's located here?"

Barnabas leaned forward to study the brown lines that indicated the old walled city of Jerusalem. "What's the date of this map?"

"As best I can determine, somewhere between the years zero and seventy. At any rate, before the destruction of the Temple." His finger was still hovering.

Barnabas said, "You have a big finger. Is it over the Garden Tomb, or the Damascus Gate?"

Libni's smile widened. "The gate."

Frustrated, Barnabas said, "I'm tired of guessing. Just tell me."

Libni's gaze scanned the shadows before he murmured, "The Square of the Column."

Barnabas blinked. Just inside the Damascus Gate there had been a broad plaza. In the middle of that plaza had stood a tall column that served as a reference point for the measurement of road distances.[1] Many groups of laborers had devised plays on that column. The one that particularly interested Libni was the form used by the stoneworkers, the *tektons,* which appeared as a builder's square tented over a circle, or column.

"And how," Barnabas inquired, "does the Square of the Column relate to..." His voice faded as the answer became obvious, and a hollow floating sensation of elation possessed him.

Libni leaned back in his chair and chuckled.

In a hushed voice, Barnabas said, "The Square of the Column marked the crossroads of the sacred city, so you think..." He paused to consider before he finished. "You think the cross on the papyrus might refer to the Crossroads?"

Libni made an airy gesture with his hand. "It explains the extra 'arms' on the basic symbol: they're roads. And it's as good a hypothesis as anything else I've come up with over the years, and not nearly as wild as some of my ideas."

For the first time in months, Barnabas saw a tiny pinprick of light shining through the dark veil of the papyrus, and he could feel his soul take another silent, measured step into the dark Chamber of Hewn Stone.

He leaned forward, slapped Libni's shoulders, and laughed, "Oh, my dear friend, how I've missed you."

5

K alay jerked awake in the darkness and glimpsed Tiras and Uzziah standing guard just inside the rounded cave entry. Their presence, however, did little to soothe her. They didn't have any weapons. What were they supposed to do if attacked? Scream? She gripped the long, curved knife in her hand all the more tightly.

The wind had dwindled to a distant whimper and the night air was thick with the smell of the sea. She inhaled deeply, but the waves of shakiness wrought by the nightmares did not go away. She couldn't shove the frightening images from her mind. Finally, she looked over at Cyrus.

He lay within reach, flat on his back, his hand on his sword. His chest rose and fell in the deep rhythms of sleep, and she was glad for him. Across the room, Zarathan slept like a child, with his straggly blond hair hanging over his eyes. His snores resembled the troubled breathing of an infant. He appeared to be in a cocoon, so tightly was he rolled in his blanket.

Kalay shook her head. If they had to rise quickly, he would still be wallowing on the floor trying to disentangle himself from his blanket when the killer cut his throat with one clean stroke. Didn't he ever think of such things?

She pondered that and decided the answer was "probably not." He'd led a soft, warm life with caring parents, always safe and well fed. A life she envied with all her heart.

As she closed her eyes and tried to force herself to sleep, a queer dread filtered through her. Once again, she found herself back in Caesarea—her parents freshly dead, fighting for garbage against fierce stray dogs whose eyes were as hungry as her own, dodging cart wheels as wagons thundered down the dirty streets, running from the smiles of men...and looking, always looking, for her brother. No matter where she went in the city, she expected to see him walking around a corner with his new family. Or maybe he'd escaped and was hiding as she was, struggling to eat. If only she could find him, they could be a family again, and—

She jerked awake when a gentle hand touched her hair.

"Are you all right?" Cyrus whispered.

"I was asleep. Why did you wake me?" she asked, her heart pounding in her throat.

He stared at her with kind eyes. "You were crying. I thought you might be having a bad dream."

Kalay blinked and discovered her cheeks were wet. She hastily wiped the tears away. "I'm fine."

"What were you dreaming?"

"Nothing. I—I don't recall."

He softly said, "Sleep, Kalay. Uzziah and Tiras will warn us if anything is amiss. We must sleep."

"I know."

She laid her head down and discovered that he had not moved his hand; it still rested comfortingly against her hair. She didn't roll away, just focused on the moon-silvered edge of his sword where it rested between them. With a light touch, Cyrus stroked her hair.

And she longed for nothing more than to lie in his arms and sleep for a month.

Her fear was more than just the nightmares, more than the utter terror of their situation, of being on the run, chased by a man who might capture and keep her alive for months or years, or until she managed to hang herself. She had begun to fear solving the riddle of the papyrus.

In a bare whisper, she asked, "Cyrus, are you afraid of what we'll find when we reach the end of this journey?"

His hand went still.

Tiras turned to look at them with wide, unblinking eyes, as though he'd heard and was as interested in the answer as she was.

Cyrus murmured, "No. But I fear what we will have to do afterward."

Kalay stared at the dark ceiling.

Afterward?

The very idea struck her as strange beyond belief. Cyrus was worried about what they would say and do after they recovered the Pearl...or failed to recover it. For her, only one question mattered: Would they live or die?

She tucked her knife beneath the edge of her blanket and listened to the night. Outside, waves washed the shore, as they had since the beginning of time, totally unconcerned with the fears of men.

MASSA—NISAN THE 14TH, THE ELEVENTH HOUR OF NIGHT

I wait in the dark courtyard just outside the high priest's palace. Less than a half hour ago, Kaiaphas summoned me and charged me with relaying the Council's decisions to the praefectus. I feel sick to my stomach. More than anything, I long to rush into the palace, free Yeshua, and make a mad dash to escape.

Laughter rises, and I glance to my right where the Roman decuria stands. It will escort Yeshua to the Praetorium where he will stand before Praefectus Pontios Pilatos. The ten soldiers talk and smile, apparently oblivious to the danger of the duty they are about to perform. To them he is just another Ioudaios, just another Jew.

My gaze drifts to the thirty Temple police officers who are stationed around the courtyard. Kaiaphas, clearly, is taking no chances.

The sound of feet upon stone echoes from inside the palace.

The massive doors swing open and two guards bring Yeshua out. He has his hands bound in front of him. Dark curly hair sticks out around the edges of the white himation pulled over his head. His eyes resemble black bonfires.

I start to go to him, but the Roman decurion, in charge of his decuria, shouts in Greek, "Stay back. No one is allowed to speak with the prisoner."

I back up, and Yeshua sucks in a breath as though to fortify himself for what is ahead.

The soldiers surround him and the decurion orders, "March to the Praetorium."

I follow along behind, escorted by two officers of the Temple police.

Pilatos's Praetorium is a magnificent structure situated on the crest of the western hill in the upper city. From the rooftop, he has a view of the sacrificial altar in the Temple compound. This pleases him. He takes every opportunity to remind the priests that he literally has his eye on them. As well, he loves the fact that one hundred years ago, his Praetorium served as the ancient royal palace for the Jewish Hasmonean kings.[1]

As I walk due east along the road, I can see the Praetorium. Built in a huge square with a massive tower at each corner, it resembles nothing so much as a luxurious fortress.

The soldiers have gone quiet, but the sound of their boots on the cobblestones echoes from the low, flat-topped houses of the poor that line the road. Here and there dogs sleep before doors. Some growl or bark at us as we pass. People are just beginning to rise, and the scent of wood smoke from breakfast fires rides the wind.

Lamps gleam in many windows. Often, I see a face staring out at us.

As we climb the western hill, my breathing grows deeper. Seven years ago, because of my language skills, the Council appointed me as liaison with the praefectus. That means I have known Lucius Pontios Pilatos since he was first appointed as praefectus of Judea, three years ago. He calls me his friend, and insists we address each other by our first names. I think it amuses him. But I know him for what he is: a brutal, shrewd man, capable of extreme cruelty. He can smell weakness and eats weak men alive. And he has contempt for all Jews. No matter what I'm feeling, I must appear to be strong.

We climb the steps to the gate and the Praetorian Guards gesture for the decuria to enter the courtyard. Broad and filled with palms and olive trees, it is a beautiful and fragrant place, especially at this tranquil hour of night.

The decuria continues walking, but my legs freeze when I see men moving in nearly every lamp-lit window. And there are more soldiers standing in the shadows against the walls of the courtyard. Panic seizes me. If I had to guess, I'd say that there are five hundred men or more here—an entire Roman cohort. There are already three cohorts stationed around the city. Did Pilatos call in this additional cohort because he feared rioting over the holy days? Why wasn't the Council informed?

I hurry to catch up with the decuria as it continues across the courtyard to the hall of judgment where two soldiers stand guard outside the door.

Before we enter, I say to the Temple officers,

"Remain outside in case I have reports I wish you to carry back to the high priest."

"Yes, Councilor."

I follow the decurion through the doors and into the hall of judgment. Despite the gleam of dozens of lamps, it is a stark place, very white, filled with white limestone, white marble, and white plastered porticos. Even Lucius Pontios Pilatos is dressed in a white toga. He stands near the Secretarium, the secret chamber where hearings and trials are held. Two of his apparitores, clerks, stand nearby. Pilatos is tall, muscular, with a swarthy complexion and hard black eyes. His closely trimmed black hair makes his clean-shaven face seem severely triangular. He has a cup of wine in one hand, and a report of some kind in the other. He's reading.

"Salve, Praefectus," I greet and bow.

"Ioses of Arimathaia, a pleasant morning to you," he says without taking his eyes from the scroll. "Are you well?"

I straighten. "Well enough. Do you know why I am here?"

He lowers the scroll and looks at me. "Yes. I was surprised when Kaiaphas sent word that you would relay the Council's decisions. Knowing, as they must, that you are a devoted follower of the accused." He holds out a hand to Yeshua.

For a moment, I cannot speak or even move. While the Council does not know it, I should not be surprised that Pilatos does.

I say, "You pay your spies far too much, Lucius. Surely they have better things to do than follow me around."

Lucius smiles. "You? Why would I follow you? My

spies follow subversives and malcontents. You're not one of those, are you?"

I gruffly fold my arms. "What if I am? Would it scare you very much?"

He laughs. "Only if I see you riding into the city tomorrow on an ugly little ass with a filthy, screaming throng behind you. Then, yes, of course, that would tremble the very foundations of Rome." He gives me a mock tremble for effect. He's enjoying himself.

I return to the issue at hand. "Lucius, being his follower does not, I believe, disqualify me from relaying the Council's decisions."

"No, of course not. I didn't mean to suggest that it did, only that they must trust you very much. Were I in their situation, I would fear that you might not relay my words accurately. Would you like a cup of wine?"

"You're very gracious, but no."

"Water, perhaps?"

"I am fine for the moment."

Pilatos shrugs and sips his wine. The cup is a work of art. Around the lip is a row of red Roman soldiers carrying shields and wearing bronze helmets. The detail is stunning. I can see the individual designs on each of the shields.

Pilatos casually asks, "It is true, is it not, that your people are forbidden to leave their houses beginning at sundown tonight?"

"When two witnesses have counted three stars, yes, Praefectus."

"And it is a grave crime if they disobey this law?"

"It is."

Pilatos smiles deprecatingly. "Then surely all will be quiet tonight. After the excessive noise, and all the *shoving and pushing in the markets, I shall look forward to that."*

He stares at me, smiles, then signals for his clerk to refill his cup of wine. As the clerk obliges, I wonder what he's up to. He never asks a question idly, and he knows Jewish laws for Pesach almost as well as I do. He's been here for three Pesach feasts.

Suspiciously, I say, "It will be quiet. Unless you are planning to stir up trouble. Is that why you have an entire cohort living in your palace?"

"Me? Cause trouble? You mean by executing your pathetic little bastard friend over there? Would that cause a riot? Or should I say, another riot?"

The guards have backed away, leaving Yeshua standing alone in the amber gleam of lamplight. He seems to be staring into some faraway kingdom, and not much liking what he sees.

My stomach muscles clench. "Yeshua ben Pantera is greatly beloved by almost everyone, as was evidenced by his rapturous welcome a few days ago when he rode into the city on his, as you say, 'ugly little ass.' And Rome, as you know, is hated by almost everyone. Surely you don't want to risk provoking a revolt."

"And surely you are not suggesting that I ignore treason."

I lift my chin. "Praefectus, the Council of Seventy-one met for most of the night. We interrogated Yeshua ben Pantera and examined witnesses. We found no evidence of treason. In fact, the witnesses agreed on almost nothing. If you have other evidence, we would very much appreciate the chance to review it."

Straightforwardly, Pilatos says, "I have two witnesses

who, in separate interrogations, implicated him in acts of treason against Rome."

"Honorable men?"

"Despicable men. Zecdots. They killed three of my soldiers earlier this week in the riot that occurred near the Temple. I condemned them to death, of course, but during their lengthy floggings they named ben Pantera as one of their supporters. Indeed, I suspect he caused the disturbance to provide a distraction that allowed the Zealots to attack my men."

I am stunned by this accusation. "What are the names of these Zealots?"

"Dysmas and Gestas. Both are from the Galilaian... as I believe your friend is."

I do not even blink. "Being from the same region is hardly a crime, Lucius. Did these Zealots say that Yeshua ben Pantera was a member of their movement, or that he agreed to help them—"

"Am I mistaken that one of his disciples is called 'Shimon the Zealot'? My sources tell me that's his name. But perhaps that's inaccurate." He waits for me to answer, knowing what I must say.

"You are not mistaken, Praefectus, but—"

"And what about the one called Yudah Sicarius? Is he not called by that name because he is a member of the dagger-wielding group known as the sicarii?"

My heart is thundering, but I lift my brows in exaggerated surprise. "You've become quite a scholar, Lucius. What's your point?"

He grins. "My point is that ben Pantera openly welcomes the enemies of Rome into his ranks."

"That says very little. He also welcomes lepers, tax

collectors, and women. It doesn't matter who they are or what they believe so long as—"

"Ioses, did you know there is a large Zealot camp hiding out in the Kidron valley, only a few steps from where your friend ben Pantera has been living with his pitiful disciples? You might as well say they've been living together."

Blood drains from my face and I feel suddenly cold. Naturally, I know. The Council makes a point of knowing such things. "I heard something, yes. Why?"

"I just found it interesting. But I'm sure that despite their loud cries for the overthrow of Rome, the Zealots are only here to celebrate the holy days, or you, my good friend, would have warned me." He sips his wine, watching me over the rim of his cup.

The soldiers around the room whisper to each other and stare hard at me. Several lower their hands to their belted daggers.

I say, "Do you have information that they plan an attack?"

He thrusts his scroll out for his clerk to take, then exhales hard. "You asked what evidence I have of ben Pantera's treason. During their floggings, the two Zealots told me that ben Pantera likened conquering Rome to a very valuable 'Pearl,' and said they should forsake even their families to obtain it. He told them he would welcome their help." Pilatos makes an airy gesture with his wine. "I call that treason. What do you call it?"

Faint tendrils of understanding are twining around my heart, crushing it. Pilatos is a clever politician. Surely he has been considering for some time the best way to be rid of the Zealots.

"I call it lies."

Pilatos's smile fades. "You admire him. I know that, but try to see this through my eyes. When a man stands so accused, three courses of action are open to me: I can find him guilty and sentence him, I can find him not guilty and acquit him, or I can decide the case has not been proven and ask that further evidence be produced. Of course, if the accused confesses, that solves the matter. So, let us proceed and see which way these proceedings go. Decurion, bring Yeshua ben Pantera into the Secretarium."

"Yes, Praefectus."

Pilatos turns his back to me and strides into the small, curtained room where hearings and trials are conducted. I see him sit upon his sella, his seat of judgment. His white toga falls in sculpted folds around his sandaled feet. When Yeshua is brought forward into the Secretarium, the clerks pull the curtain closed for privacy and station themselves outside. The decurion backs away, and to my surprise, Pilatos's hand appears and shoves the curtain open, so that I can see him—or perhaps so he can see me.

This mystifies me. I know the rules. Once these proceedings begin, no one outside the Secretarium is allowed to speak. It's called a Secretarium *because the proceedings are supposed to be secret. Surely he can't be planning on carrying on a conversation with me. Roman law is clear:* vanae voces populi non sunt audiendae, *the vain voices of the people may not be listened to.*[2]

"Come forward," he orders Yeshua.

Yeshua kneels at Pilatos's feet.

Pilatos's brows lift, as though he suspects the gesture is an obsequious appeal for leniency. I know it is not, since I've seen Yeshua kneel before his own disciples, as well as the lame, the sick.

"They call you Rab, do they not?" Pilatos asks.[3]

Yeshua closes his eyes again and his lips move with a silent prayer.

"Shall I call you that? Rab?" Pilatos presses. "Are you a teacher? A great chief? A wise man?"

Yeshua whispers, "Everyone that is of the Truth hears my voice."

Pilatos glances at me, and hisses, "His voice, not the emperor's." He turns back to Yeshua. "I have heard many of the Ioudaiosoi say that you are the son of David. Are you a king? The king of the Jews?"

Almost forlornly, Yeshua exhales the words, "You say so."

"Is that a yes or a no? And take care in answering me, for pretending to be a king is treasonable under the Lex Julia, the Laws of Rome."

Perhaps suspecting he's walking into a trap, Yeshua wisely says nothing.

Pilatos heaves an annoyed breath. "Let me clarify so that I am sure you understand the charge. It is a capital offense known as crimen laesae maiestatis *to claim to be the king of a province under Roman rule, unless the emperor has nominated you as the king of that province, as the emperor did for your King Herod. But I do not believe you have been so nominated. Have you?"*

Yeshua replies, "My kingdom is not of this world. If it were, wouldn't my followers be fighting for my release right now? I came into this world to bear witness to the Truth."

"I didn't ask about the bravery of your so-called followers, I asked if you were a king. I assume if you

have a kingdom—wherever it is—then you claim to be a king. Is that correct?"

Yeshua stays silent.

Pilatos's dark brows plunge down. "Perhaps I have misunderstood your answer. Are you telling me that you are not a king in a political sense, but rather in a theological, moral sense?"

Yeshua's mouth tightens."[4]

Pilatos turns to me. "Ioses, surely you see that pretensions such as this make his offense all the more grave. He claims that his kingdom is not comprised of this puny little remote province, but is divine and universal. He has set himself and his kingdom up against the divinity of the emperor and Rome. Only the kingdom of the immortal Tiberias Caesar is divine and universal."

This sends a surge of blood through my veins. Now I understand why he left the curtain open. I am his witness. He wants me to report what I have seen to the Council.

I open my mouth to object, despite the consequences, but Pilatos says, "Ioses, even if I did not have the testimonies of the Zealots regarding his treasonous words, I could not allow such contempt of the emperor to go unpunished. Surely you see that." He rises to his feet and passes sentence: "Yeshua ben Pantera, in accordance with Roman law, I find you guilty of treason against the holy Roman Empire. I sentence you to be crucified on this day, along with your conspirators Dysmas and Gestas."

Then he turns to me and smiles as he says, "Decurion, take him to his cell, and as a favor to my good friend Ioses of Arimathaia, I order you to scourge ben Pantera until he's half dead. That should hasten his death on the cross. He won't suffer so long. I'm a generous man, aren't I, Ioses?"[5]

The decurion waves his soldiers forward and they surround Yeshua and march him away. [6]

A stinging sensation filters through my body. I feel light-headed. Somewhere deep inside me a voice keeps saying, no, no, no...

Pilatos glances at me and starts to walk away.

"Praefectus, please give me a few moments to speak with you."

"You are my friend, Ioses. Of course."

I can barely stand, and he smiles as though the morning has been a trifling matter.

"By Jewish law and custom, we must bury our dead before nightfall on a feast day. I humbly request the right to take down and bury each man who dies today."

The God of Yisrael demands that I show the same generosity of spirit for the other two criminals that I do for Yeshua. And Yeshua...Yeshua would expect that what I do for the man whom I love, I also do for the strangers whom I know not."[7]

"But Ioses, you know it is Roman law that a crucified man may not be buried. Such bodies are to be left on the cross until beasts and birds of prey devour them. We even post guards to make certain that friends or family members cannot take down a corpse. In fact, unauthorized burial of a crucified criminal is a crime."[8]

"Yes, I—I know that. But we both also know that the emperor or his officers may grant special authorization to bury such a convict. You yourself have given such permission on occasion. I'm asking that you, once again, grant a special dispensation to allow me to bury them."

An expression of annoyance creases his lean, dark

face. *"If these Zealots had been convicted by the Council of Seventy-one, what would happen to their corpses?"*

I wonder why he's asking. He couldn't care less what happens to Jews. "It is against the law for any person to bury or mourn a criminal executed by a Jewish court. Such convicts are buried by the court in the court's graveyard, outside the city walls."[9]

Pilatos frowns, as though thinking. "Then if I grant you a special burial permit, I will appear particularly generous, won't I?"

"Oh, yes, very generous. And I assure you the Council will be deeply grateful."

Pilatos signals to his dark-haired clerk and as the young man rushes across the room, he says, "Write out a burial permit for Ioses of Arimathaia."[10]

"For all three convicts?" *the clerk asks.*

"Yes, all three, providing they die today. But—" *Pilatos adds,* "bring me the nails."

"Yes, Praefectus."

Pilatos gives him a cold smile, says, " Valete, Ioses," *then turns and walks away.*

The clerk says, "If you will wait a few moments—"

"I will wait."

The clerk leaves.

My thoughts are disjointed, flashing from one image to the next, as though I've been struck in the head and can no longer piece together even the simplest of puzzles.

There is only one thing I know for certain: Pilatos has no idea what he's about to do. A holy man who perishes at the hands of the oppressors of Yisrael will join the ranks of heroes who, throughout history, have sacrificed their lives for the faith and paved the way for the ultimate liberation of Yisrael. He's about to turn Yeshua into a holy martyr, a man whose name other men will fight and die for. A man who, by the end of the day, every Zealot in the city will be ready to die for.

I suddenly go numb.

A breath of cool wind eddies through the hall and causes the lamps to waver and spit. Yellow light flutters over the walls.

Dear God.

A riot is just the excuse he needs to attack the Zealot camp and wipe out every last man. With the streets clear because people must remain in their houses, his legions will be able to move unheeded, to slaughter at will. And, for the first time, I know Gamliel is right.[11]

7

Loukas flattened his body against the shadowed cliff and watched the horses on the beach. They walked with their heads down, as though too tired to place one hoof in front of the other. He'd watched as Atinius and Kalay had disappeared into the cave, leaving the two inexperienced youths to guard the entrance. He'd been working his way from shadow to shadow since that time, and the young monks had not even glanced his way. Now and then they spoke to each other, but he couldn't understand their words.

He let his gaze wander to the boulders that lined the shore. From this vantage, they resembled a curving mouth filled with broken, rotting teeth.

It had taken meager effort to find this place, ten well-placed questions in the local villages. Everyone knew of Libni the Hermit, or Old Scary, though only a few knew the exact location of his caves.

Loukas motioned to his accomplices. The four men slid forward, and one by one, ghosted past him. Loukas watched with narrowed eyes. Why on earth Pappas

Athanasios had chosen these men from all of the defenders of the faith stationed in Alexandria, Loukas did not know. They were too old to be given such responsibilities. Gray shot through their short hair and eyebrows, glinting in the moonlight. And, despite their muscular frames, Loukas doubted they had the agility to respond to a well-timed assault. At least they wore black togas that blended with the darkness. That would give them a small edge.

Not that it mattered. They had one purpose here tonight. To Loukas it seemed ludicrous. All the more so since his second humiliation at the hands of Atinius in Leontopolis. He needed but reach down to remind himself of the wound to his manhood and pride.

I just hope this new plan of yours works, Meridias.

For a long time, Loukas's world consisted of standing with his back pressed against the damp, cold stone, watching the Egyptians' slow advance, and straining to hear.

Despite his desperate need to watch Atinius bleed, and to wring terror from that she-devil of a woman, he would follow orders.

He always had.

8

It was still the middle of the night when Kalay awoke, stirred, and combed tangled hair out of her eyes. For a blank moment, she couldn't remember where she was; this was *not* her washing hut. Where the dank, muddy odor of the Nile should have been, the scent of the sea confused her...then a flurry of hushed voices sent her scrambling for her knife. In a flash, she'd thrown off her blanket and rolled against the wall, Loukas's long, curving blade clutched in her fist.

The unearthly glow of starlight through thick fog turned the world murky, and she saw the dark shapes of three men near the cave mouth. The tallest, Cyrus, was little more than a black ghost, moving along the wall toward the entrance. One of the shapes—Tiras, she thought—edged into the tunnel that led to the library and vanished.

Near the entrance, there was the startled snort of a horse and a flurry of pounding hooves.

Kalay felt her insides shrivel. She pulled herself to a squat and held her breath.

She could no longer see Cyrus. He had blended into the darkness. Was he by the entrance?

From somewhere outside a man said, "Centurion? You can't escape. Give up now. Surrender the papyrus, and you'll save the lives of your companions. Trying to stand against us is useless. I have a full garrison out here."

Not Loukas. Nonetheless, a thousand years from now, her moldering bones would recognize that cold, insidious voice.

A black shadow wavered near the entrance.

Cyrus said, "I don't think so. If you did, twenty men would have already rushed this cave and dragged us out. Since they didn't, I assume you're either alone, or have but a few men with you."

Turning her head slightly, she looked across the room and made out Zarathan, still fast asleep.

Dear Iesous Christos, the stupidest killer in the world could creep up on him and crush his skull.

The man outside moved...and she saw him. He stood with his back pressed against the stone just beyond the lip of the cave. There was another man behind him, shorter, with a wealth of gray hair that glimmered in the starlight.

Kalay gestured to Cyrus, held up two fingers, then pointed to where they stood. She had no idea if he could see her or not, but his black shadow moved another step closer to the entrance. He slid his hand into the light, lifted one finger, and pointed to her side of the entrance.

The fear pumping in her veins almost made her sick. She rose to a crouch and moved into position.

From this perspective, she could see the men

clearly. Both were dressed in black, but their swords glinted wetly, appearing and disappearing in the wind-blown shreds of fog.

The cave suddenly felt stifling; fear sweat matted her dress to her body. Fighting to keep her breathing even, she leaned her shoulder against the stone wall.

"I have been authorized to make you an offer," the tall man called.

"What offer?"

"The Church is willing to pardon all of you. You need only surrender the papyrus and take vows of silence."

She saw Cyrus shake his head as though incredulous and heard his low laugh. "Tell Pappas Meridias that there is no 'papyrus.' And of what use is such a guarantee? On the Church's orders, Meridias murdered an entire monastery...almost one hundred monks who had devoted their lives to God. What are seven more lives?"

The men skulked closer, close enough that Kalay could see their pale faces.

"Centurion, we know that you are the only one in there with fighting skills. If you don't surrender, all of your friends will die because of you. Is that what you want?"

Despite her best efforts, her breathing had gone low and ragged, hissing through her nostrils.

On the far side of the cave, three quiet shadows emerged from the tunnel and took up positions around the walls. The sound of their footsteps was barely audible. They might have been soldiers rather than monks.

Kalay heard fabric grate on stone outside and knew they were moving in for the kill.

She gripped her knife in her right hand and held it low, ready to lunge and rip upward. By the age of fifteen, she'd learned you never raised a knife over your head. A man could grab your wrist, twist, and take it away from you with little effort. It was harder to block a knife if it was held low and close. Problem was, if they came in with swords swinging, she'd lose her hands long before she had a chance to attack.

Cyrus looked directly at Kalay. He mouthed the word, "Ready?"

She jerked a nod.

Just as Cyrus lifted his sword...

A wild, inhuman shriek rose from the rear of the cave, congealing the blood in Kalay's veins. Before she could force her shaking legs to move, a mountainous vision of fluttering brown rags rushed past her and out into the thick fog.

Barnabas cried, "Libni, no!"

After a heartbeat's hesitation, Cyrus, Barnabas, Tiras, and Uzziah charged out behind Libni. The metallic clashing of swords erupted, along with screams.

Kalay girded herself and eased out into the moonlit mist, trying to see what was happening. She glimpsed swirling figures, flashes of swords, and saw that the battle was moving south, down the beach.

She took two running steps to follow ...

A big black-gloved hand thrust out of the mist, caught her sleeve, and wrenched her off her feet. She hit the ground hard, kicking and flailing, roaring in anger, until she saw the sword blade drop through the fog and stop just above her heart.

"Move, and you're dead," the harsh voice ordered. She could hear the tension, nearly panic, behind it.

Kalay subtly tucked her knife beneath her skirt and stared up at him.

"Lie still, you little *scorta,* or I'll forgo my orders and cut you in half." The man was muscular, stalky, with gray-streaked black hair.

"What do you want with me? I don't know anything!"

A shout rose down the shore and he glanced in that direction, smiled, and boldly kneeled beside her. His gaze traveled over her throat and the swell of her breasts. With one swift jerk, he undid her belt. Ripping away the bronze dagger and purse, he tossed them aside. Then he grabbed her jaw in his gloved hand and wrenched her face to look at it. "Now I see why he wants you alive. You're a pretty thing."

"Who? Who wants me?" A fiery rush flushed her veins.

"Get on your feet, and let's go. He's waiting for you." The man stood up and loomed over her, his sword clutched in both hands.

Shaking and terrified, she did her best to conceal the knife as she struggled to stand up, but he must have seen a glint of silver, for he shouted, "Throw it down!" and sprang at her. His mistake was raising his sword for a strike.

In one smooth motion, Kalay stepped inside the reach of his sword, and slashed with all her strength. Her blade cut a diagonal across his chest. His tunic parted under the keen edge and she watched his flesh part in the blade's wake, could feel it vibrating across bone.

The man jerked back, bellowed in rage, and stared down at the blood welling on his chest. When he glanced up, a dazed disbelief filled his eyes. He began to circle; his sword gleamed with an unnatural fire as, bleeding badly, he raised it to strike her. She tried to fling herself aside, but didn't have time....

A hollow thunk rang out, and the killer staggered, stared at her in surprise, then toppled to the sand in a black heap. Rolling on the ground, his arms flailing, he managed to get to his hands and knees, almost stood, and dropped back to all fours.

Kalay leaped, grasped his hair, and drew her blade across his throat. His frantic exhalation blew a spray of night-dark blood across the churned sand.

The entire time, Zarathan stood shaking, clutching a driftwood club in his hand. His chalky face was sweat-drenched. When the killer finally stopped spasming and lay still, Zarathan's legs failed him. He crumpled.

"Zarathan? Are you all right?"

He hunched over and held his belly, while he rocked back and forth, sobbing like a child. "I—I didn't know wh-what else to do."

The assailant kicked one last time. Kalay glanced at him, watched for a moment, then looked back at Zarathan. "Stop crying," she said unsympathetically. "You should be happy. You just accomplished the impossible."

Confused, he looked up at her with huge tear-filled eyes. "What are you talking about? I just *killed a* man!"

"Yes, and because of that, no one will ever again say that you resemble a circumcised cat." She paused to wipe her face on her sleeve. "And, actually, I killed him, but you certainly stunned him. You're braver than I thought. I'm grateful. You saved my life."

"Brave?" he wailed. "I'm a coward! I sneaked up and struck him from behind! And now I—I can't stop crying!"

"Yes, well, the first time I killed a man, I couldn't stop throwing up."

He buried his face in his hands and made sounds like he was suffocating.

To give him time to collect himself, Kalay walked over and retrieved her belt, knotted it back around her waist, and went about picking up the Roman purse and bronze dagger. Finally, she lifted the dead man's sword. When Zarathan still hadn't stopped crying, Kalay marched over, grabbed him by the arm, forcibly dragged him to the ocean, and flung him face-first into the surf.

He came up looking like a drowned weasel, and cried, "Are you insane? Why did you do that?"

"I thought another good baptism would clear your head. You..."

Twenty paces down the shoreline she thought she glimpsed a figure, a shape moving silently in the bottomless fog. Her heart almost leaped out of her chest.

"Zarathan, stand up!" she ordered as she tested the sword's balance. "Come on!"

He got to his feet and staggered out of the water with his saturated robe clinging to his skinny frame. "What's wrong?"

The ominous figure had vanished in the fog, but she could feel him, slipping closer. The hair on her neck began to prickle.

"Quickly. Grab your club, we—"

From near the cliff, Cyrus shouted, "Kalay? Zarathan?"

"Here! We're over here!"

Footsteps pounded the sand. Kalay turned back, scanning the fog, the tip of the sword swinging in small circles as she prepared to defend herself.

But the figure was gone.

If he'd ever really been there.

Cyrus appeared out of the mist, covered in blood, hauling Libni with one hand and carrying his dripping sword with the other. "Libni is wounded. Hurry!"

9

"Find candles," Barnabas ordered Tiras. "Bring them to the library immediately."

"Yes, brother."

Tiras ran ahead of them through the dark tunnel.

Barnabas trailed along behind Cyrus. The warrior monk was virtually carrying Libni, though his old friend was making an effort to put one foot in front of the other. When they entered the library cave, Tiras had one candle lit and was placing it on the far end of the table.

Cyrus propped his sword against the wall and bodily lifted Libni onto the tabletop.

A long sword gash sliced diagonally from his collarbone to the base of his ribs. The amount of blood was disconcerting; it ran from the gaping flesh, soaked his clothing, and pooled on the table. Spatters had patterned Libni's face and throat.

Tiras, as though totally disoriented, gaped in shock.

"Tiras, bring the candle down here, please?"

The dazed youth blinked, picked up the candle, and

brought it to Barnabas, who took it from his shivering hand.

The boy had just seen his best friend, Uzziah, killed and was watching his mentor bleed to death in front of him.

"Tiras," Barnabas said gently. "Fetch a jug of water and bandages. Oh, and I will need a needle and heavy thread. I assume you have these things?"

"Yes, b-brother." Tiras turned and shouldered between Zarathan and Kalay, who'd just entered the chamber.

"Oh, dear God." Zarathan's voice was a thin wail. He put a hand to his mouth and stared wide-eyed at Libni's blood.

Cyrus didn't waste a moment. "I must go and guard the entrance. Kalay, can you gather our horses and bring them here?"

"Of course." She vanished down the tunnel at a run.

"Our horses?" Barnabas said, "Cyrus, you're not planning on leaving? Libni needs our help!"

"I know that, brother, but as soon as we've done what we can, we have to go."

"But—"

"Brother Barnabas! We killed two of our attackers. At least two ran, and it is prudent to believe that the leader was watching from a distance. Someone must carry the tale back to his superiors. By dawn, they will be on their way back here in force. We can't stay." He gestured to the gazelle leather bag sitting almost invisible on the floor in the rear of the cave. "Unless you want the papyrus to fall into the Church's hands."

"No, of course not, but—"

Libni reached out and gripped Barnabas's sleeve. "He's right. You have to go. Tiras will care for me."

"Libni, you and Tiras must come with us. It's not safe here."

Libni smiled and through a long, pained exhalation, he replied, "There are...many other caves. Near here. Very difficult to negotiate. No one knows the maze but me. We will hide there."

"No, Libni, please. You must leave. You don't know these men, they'll—"

"We will trust our fate to God and our Lord Iesous Christos. But..." He winced as he sucked in a breath. "Promise me that if you succeed you will return and tell me what you saw?" Libni's eyes shone with hope.

Barnabas took his hand in a hard grip. "You know I will."

Tiras rushed back into the cave with an armload of bandages, herbs, and a jug of water, which he deposited on the table beside Barnabas. Then he laid out a long iron needle and a ball of dark-brown thread.

Cyrus collected his blood-darkened sword, adding, "Call out if you need me."

Zarathan, sodden, stood with his shoulders hunched and a puddle forming at his feet. Wet blond hair straggled around his face.

"Zarathan," Barnabas said, "please hold the candle for me while Tiras and I tend to the wound."

Zarathan, looking as if about to faint, took the candle and held it close. Barnabas carefully peeled back the blood-slick fabric. Without realizing it, his eyes tightened, and Libni said, "Am I dying? Finally?"

"Don't be ridiculous. God still needs you. If for no other reason than to irritate me with guessing games."

Turning just slightly, he said, "Tiras, hand me the needle and thread. Once we get the bleeding stopped, I will need to sew the cut closed."

"Yes, brother."

Zarathan swallowed hard. "How do we stop the bleeding?"

"Set the candle down and press both your hands on the wound, here and here," he pointed. "Press the cut edges together. Don't let up on the pressure until I tell you to." Barnabas unwound the thread and slipped it through the eye of the needle. "Tiras, help him."

Zarathan did as instructed and Tiras pressed his hands on the other most critical gaps. Libni gritted his teeth in pain, but barely a moan escaped his lips.

It seemed to take an eternity before the blood flow began to ebb. Cautiously, Barnabas drove the needle into Libni's flesh. Not even the years of tailoring his own clothing had prepared him for this. Stitch by stitch, he closed the wound. "Let go now, Zarathan, and move down some. We'll wash it after we sew it closed."

Libni uttered a rasping groan.

"Forgive me." Barnabas continued to sew, attempting to copy the neat stitches he'd seen Roman surgeons make.

Libni vented a low laugh. His bloody face appeared ghoulish in the candlelight, especially surrounded by that mop of gore-clotted hair. "Barnabas?"

"What is it?"

Libni's voice changed. "I have a favor to ask. Can you take some of my books with you? I know they're cumbersome, but Tiras and I, we'll have to leave quickly. I don't think we'll have time to carry all of them to our hiding place."

"Yes, of course. But just the most important documents, Libni. One bag full. I'll tie it as a counterweight to the gazelle leather bag."

"Thank you, thank you." Libni winced at a sudden stab of pain and focused on the arching cave ceiling where candlelit shadows danced. Tears were leaking down the side of his blood-spattered face. "I have...have copies of the gospels of Markos, Thomas, and Maththaios in Hebrew and Aramaic. Very rare. The only copies I've ever seen."

"The only copies I've ever heard of," Barnabas said in awe. *Dear God, the implications.* Softly, he asked, "Does Markos have the longer ending?"

"No, of course not. It ends at chapter sixteen, verse eight. As it did before it was rewritten."

Barnabas glanced up at Zarathan and Tiras. Both were obviously running verses through their minds, trying to decipher the meaning.

Libni followed his gaze, saw their expressions, and said, "The oldest versions of the Gospel of Markos end at chapter sixteen, verse seven or eight. There is no resurrection."

"But," Zarathan said, "don't both Irenaeus and Hippolytus mention verse nine? They lived in the second and third centuries. Surely that proves—"

"It proves that even then men were using their pens to mutilate the original gospels," Libni said gruffly. "Myth-making at the cost of history. It's disgraceful. My Hebrew and Aramaic gospels date to the latter half of the first century. They were written only a few decades after our Lord was crucified. And my Hebrew Gospel of Thomas dates to around the year 40, maybe 50 at the latest. I think it was written before the letters of Paulos. Take them with you, Barnabas. Don't let the Church editors get their grubby nibs near them."

"I won't. I swear it." But he wondered how, if they were captured, he would be able to keep that promise.

As he worked his way across the wound, the blood ceased to flow, but he could see Libni's face going more and more pale, probably a combination of shock and loss of blood. He took his last stitch, tied it off, and said, "Tiras, find every blanket here. We need to keep Libni warm while he sleeps."

Tiras hurried from the room.

"But aren't we leaving soon?" Zarathan asked hopefully.

Barnabas smiled down into Libni's pained eyes. "As soon as we've gathered whatever books Libni tells us to."

Libni gave him a weak smile, sealing a bargain that the protection of the original gospels was passing from one trusted friend to another. What was at stake was no more, and no less, than the Truth.

Libni lifted a shaking hand and pointed to the small hole in the wall on the right side of the cave. "Thomas is there, and Markos..." His finger moved through the air to a large, squarish hole. "Markos and Maththaios are there. But there are others. An early version of Hebrews and the second volume of Papias's *Logia*..."

Tiras returned and began piling blankets atop Libni while he continued with his list.

For nearly an hour, Barnabas and Zarathan collected and carefully packed the ancient papyri, scrolls, and codices into a cracked leather bag Tiras had found.

Finally, Libni allowed himself to fall into a deep, exhausted sleep.

Barnabas backed away from the table and motioned for Tiras to follow them out.

When they stood on the sand, Barnabas said, "Zarathan, please take both bags to our horse and tie them over the withers."

"Yes, brother."

Barnabas turned to Tiras. The youth gazed up at him with terrified eyes, as though he longed for nothing more than to run away and hide from all this.

"Tiras, remember that 'there is light within a man of light, and he lights the whole world. If that man does not shine, he is the darkness,'[1] and he will not find the Kingdom." He put his hand on the youth's shoulder. "Shine, Tiras. Be a man of light, as he taught you."

Tears welled in Tiras's eyes. He nodded and reverently said, "I will try, brother. Don't worry. I'll take care of him."

"I know you will."

Barnabas turned and strode for the horses.

10

Z arathan helped Cyrus adjust the book bags over the horse's withers, while he cast occasional glances at Kalay. The woman kneeled by the dead assassin, going through his pockets. She'd rinsed her bloody face and hair in the sea, but there were still dark splotches on her dress.

Solemnly, Cyrus said, "Kalay told me you saved her life. Thank you, brother. I know it was a hard thing to do."

Zarathan's gaze pulled back, and he anxiously toyed with the ropes on the bags. What could he say? His wrists ached from the panicked strength of the blow he'd wielded, but it was nothing compared to the pain that seemed to live and breathe in his heart.

Despite what Kalay said, I killed him. Without my blow, he would be alive.

In a soft, confidential voice, Cyrus asked, "Are you all right?"

He had never known why, but he found it difficult to share grief, even with his family.

Cautiously, he said, "Cyrus, you—you're a soldier. You probably think I'm a weak fool. And I—I am." He hated the frail timbre of the words. "But I've never been in a fight before, not even with my fists. Every time I got into a situation that looked like it might turn ugly, I walked away—as I believe my Lord wants me to do."

"I believe he does, too, brother." Cyrus adjusted the bags for a final time, and the smell of the sea seemed to grow sharper, more intense.

Zarathan wiped his nose on his wet sleeve. "I acted like a coward. I didn't even fight the man face-to-face. I sneaked up on him and clubbed him from behind!"

Cyrus rested his arms across the horse's back. His thick black brows drew down over his straight nose. "Zarathan, these men are trying to kill us. Always, whenever possible, attack from behind. The goal is for you to come out alive. Use whatever tactics you must to accomplish that."

"Including acting like a coward?"

Cyrus considered him. "Had you called him out, faced him man-to-man, what would have happened?"

"He would have killed me."

"That's right. He was skilled in arms, you are not. He would have lopped your head off with one stroke and then turned and finished Kalay. You would both be dead, and he would have been there to turn the odds against me and in our attackers' favor. Which means that Brother Barnabas, Libni, Tiras, and I would be dead, too. And, at this moment, the papyrus and all the books would be burning."

"But..." He suppressed a sob. "If what I did was right, why do I feel so horrible?"

A bitter smile turned Cyrus's lips. "I executed my

first man when I was your age, Zarathan. Sixteen. They called it 'military training.' My commander brought me an enemy soldier who'd been taken prisoner in battle. He was a barbarian, filthy—and he was trussed up like a hog ready for roasting. It certainly wasn't a fair fight."

Zarathan managed to get a shaky breath into his lungs. "What did you do?"

"I was ordered to slice off his head, and I really tried to obey. I lifted my sword several times. But each time I looked into his pleading eyes, and I couldn't do it. When I broke down in tears, my commander ordered the other recruits to beat me until I either begged to go home to my mother, or until I begged to kill the prisoner."

There was a long silence while Cyrus patted the horse's mane; his eyes were lost in distant memories. Barnabas ducked out of the cave, and walked toward them with his head bowed, as though beneath a great weight.

"Did you kill the prisoner?" Zarathan asked.

"Oh, yes."

"And af-afterward? Did you feel weak all over? As though your muscles had been boiled until they felt like they would fall apart?"

"I still feel that way when I kill a man. I don't think good soldiers ever get over it. Killing is wrong. We all know it. I don't know God's reason for it, but there are times, my brother, when it simply cannot be avoided. Like today."

Zarathan chewed his lip while he looked out at the frothy surf.

Cyrus softly said, "You weren't a coward tonight. You were braver than I was when I first killed a man.

You knew what you had to do, and did it without thinking, without hesitating. From now on, I know I can rely upon you when the time comes."

Several hollow thuds echoed down the beach, and they both turned to see Kalay level yet another brutal kick at the dead man's privates.

Baffled and annoyed, Zarathan said, "I still think she's a demon."

Cyrus studied Kalay. "Don't forget that our Lord sent her into the dining hall that night at the monastery. Then he placed her in the boat with us. And tonight he had you pick up that piece of driftwood to save her life." His eyes softened. "There must be a reason."

11

MASSA—NISAN THE 17TH, THE YEAR 3771

Yosef slipped the bit into his horse's mouth and patted the animal's silken neck as he secured the bridle. The horse blew and looked at him with big, trusting eyes.

"Just two more days, Adolphus," he said gently. "Then you'll be able to spend the rest of your life grazing in fields of green grass. I promise."

All around him, the Essenes were busy, packing their horses, cleaning up camp, speaking in low voices. He looked out across the silent, dove-colored hills to the highlands in the distance. As sunlight broke over the horizon, a tawny gleam haloed the place where the Holy City of Yerushalaim nestled. He thought of his home, the home he suspected he could never again return to, and a pained yearning struck his heart. He so wanted to sleep in his own bed, and to see his ailing father one last time. Perhaps, if Petronius...

No, you can't let yourself believe that. It will weaken

your resolve. You have one duty left to perform, then you must flee.

He patted the horse again, gripped the reins, and led Adolphus toward the other horses; his hooves clip-clopped across the stone in a slow, patient rhythm.

Mattias called, "We're ready if you are."

"Good. Let's ride."

Either they would find Titus waiting for them tonight at the prearranged place, or they would not, which meant he'd been captured and the Pearl stolen.

Regardless, someone would be waiting for them.

He prayed it wasn't an entire Roman century.

12

MELEKIEL—NISAN THE L8TH, FIRST HOUR OF NIGHT

By the time they neared the city of Emmaus,[1] the sun had long ago dipped below the western horizon, and the broadside stars glittered to life.

Yosef galloped his horse in the lead, following the twisting path through the fruit orchard. The fragrance of green leaves and last year's rotting pomegranates carried on the breeze.

When he saw the dilapidated house ahead, his heart ached, for he did not see Titus.

Mattias galloped up beside him and hissed, "Where is he?" Sweat-soaked black hair clung to his cheeks.

"I don't know, but I pray he's alive. Where are your brothers?"

"They're watching the main road."

Yosef said, "Stay here. I'm going in alone."

"But why? You may need me."

"If this is a trap, someone must ride back and warn your brothers, or they too will be caught and executed."

Mattias stared at him, then nodded. "You're right. I'll wait here."

Yosef reined his horse to within twenty paces of the house and cautiously dismounted. "Titus?" he called. Then a little more loudly, "Titus? Are you here?"

The only sound was the breeze whistling through the gaps in the collapsed roof.

He impatiently tied Adolphus to an overgrown bush and walked toward the dark house. From the smell, the building had recently been used as a barn. The scents of manure and moldering hay were strong.

As he peered in one of the windows, his nerves stretched to the breaking point. He couldn't keep his hands still.

He walked to the door. Inside, he could see fallen roof beams, broken pots, and piles of windblown debris. "Titus?"

Wind shoved a loose board, and when it creaked mournfully, Yosef jerked his knife from the sheath and froze. Along the wall to his right, tiny, glistening eyes flashed as mice scurried for cover.

He listened for any other sound.

Then he stepped into the house, edged around a pile of sheep manure, and tiptoed toward the closed door in the rear. "Titus?"

He pushed the door open and entered. Blackness. When he and Titus had last been here three years ago, this had been a storage room. The faint fragrances of dried fruits and herbs temporarily overpowered that of the manure and mildew.

As Yosef groped along the wall to his left, he

94

bumped against an old crate. Then his hand touched another wall and he felt his way toward the wall niche he remembered—the curtained niche where the farmer had stored his family's most precious items. When his hand brushed a rotted piece of cloth, then sank into the wall, he knew he'd found it.

For five rapid heartbeats, he just stood there, praying. Then he stuck his hand deeper into the niche and felt around. Nothing. Just thick dust and spiderwebs.

Yosef pulled his hand out and sank against the wall. There was no message. Titus had not been here. At least not yet, and if he hadn't already arrived, there was a good chance he never would. Though Titus must have been forced to hide out for hours or even a day, he would not have lingered anywhere, knowing as he did that time was of the essence.

Yosef's despair was so overpowering, he barely noticed the tiny creak in the outer room. As the night cooled, wood contracted and the small animals began to emerge from their hiding places in search of food...

The next time he heard it, he looked up and focused on the ajar door.

The third time, he crouched down behind a toppled cupboard and gripped his knife in a hard fist.

Just above a whisper, a man called, "Master?"

"Titus!"

Yosef lunged for the door, threw it open, and ran straight into the arms of four Roman soldiers. Dressed in common brown robes, they had clean-shaven faces and carried the *gladii*, the short swords, of the Legion. Two of them held Titus by the arms. He was filthy and sweating profusely. His face and brown curly hair were covered with dust and streaks of soot.

"Throw down your knife!" the tall blond man said and aimed his sword at Yosef. He had an almost feminine oval face with long lashes, but the muscles that bulged through his robe spoke of many battles.

Yosef tossed the knife to the floor and held up his hands.

"Forgive me, Master," Titus said in a shaking voice. "I arrived only moments before you and found them waiting for me."

"Then..."

Neither of them had to say it.

They have the Pearl.

Titus's chest heaved with silent sobs.

The officer said, "I am Centurion Lutatius Crassus, here by order of Praefectus Pontios Pilatos. You are under arrest."

"On what charge?" Yosef asked.

"Come with us." The officer led the way out the door and the men holding Titus forced him to follow. The remaining soldier used his sword to gesture for Yosef to follow Titus.

With his hands up, he stepped out into the dusk, where four more soldiers stood guard.

The surrounding orchards had turned dark and foreboding, but the sky continued to gleam with a faint purplish hue.

Centurion Crassus strode out into the trees and, as Yosef fell into line behind Titus, he saw eight horses grazing placidly amid the fruit trees. Titus's packhorse was tied to a low branch with the linen-wrapped bundle still on its back; it looked intact.

Hope rose up to choke him.

Perhaps, if one of them could create a diversion, the other could...

The centurion walked straight to the horse, used his knife to cut the straps, and shoved the heavy linen bundle to the ground. Yosef let out a small cry of shock, and tried to run forward, but his guard shouted, "Stop or I'll kill you!"

Yosef's steps faltered. He stood trembling as tears filled his eyes.

"What is this?" the officer asked, pointing at the bundle with his sword.

Titus and Yosef glanced at each other, but neither answered.

Grumbling, the officer bent down and ripped at the linen with his sword, shredding it. He ripped again, only to stop when a human arm flopped out. The sword had cut a wide gash across the wrist. Bloodless, it gaped open like a ragged violet mouth.

For a moment, Yosef was so stunned, he couldn't speak. He could clearly see the man's right hand. What had happened to his ring? His grandfather's ring? He'd placed it on the index finger himself, he knew for certain...

"Are you aware," the centurion said, "that it is a crime to steal the body of a crucified criminal?"

Yosef's eyes blurred. The world took on a blinding shimmer.

The centurion kicked the bundle over and tugged hard to unwrap the linen. When the body rolled out, Yosef couldn't help it, a sob choked him and tears traced warm lines down his cheeks. If he lived to be a thousand, he would never forget this terrible, wrenching moment. He felt like his heart had been ripped out.

The centurion stared down, then straightened. "You"—he gestured to Yosef—"come forward and identify this man."

Guards escorted Yosef to the body. He looked down, and his knees went weak.

In stunned confusion, he stammered, "It—it's Dysmas. D-Dysmas the Zealot."

"That's what I thought. I was sent to arrest you for the theft of the body of the criminal known as Yeshua ben Pantera, but this is not his body."

Yosef glanced at Titus, silently asking what he'd done, but Titus violently shook his head.

The centurion appeared perturbed. "Where is the body of ben Pantera?"

Yosef shrugged. "I do not know, Centurion. That's the truth."

The officer scowled at Titus. "Where is the body?"

"I don't know what you're talking about! We promised that when the holy days were over, we would get Dysmas's body to his family in Ioppe. My master received a special permit from the praefectus himself to bury this man! Now..." He swallowed his tears and waved to the body. "Now, his body has been violated, mutilated! I can't face his mother."

Yosef longed to kiss him.

Crassus sheathed his sword and propped his hands on his hips as he glared at Yosef. "You are Ioses of Arimathaia, yes?"

"I am."

"High Priest Kaiaphas told the praefectus that after you'd placed ben Pantera's body in your tomb, he'd had you imprisoned to prevent you from doing something foolish, like stealing the body and proclaiming your friend had fulfilled Jewish prophecies. Were you imprisoned?"

It was against the law for Romans to interfere in the actions of the Council of Seventy-one, unless the Council requested their assistance. Yosef was praying it had not.

Yosef wiped his eyes on his sleeve. "I was not imprisoned by Roman order, Centurion, therefore you have no jurisdiction over my escape. Do you? Are you here to enforce the orders of the Council of Seventy-one?"

Crassus's mouth pursed disdainfully. "I do not enforce Jewish orders."

"Then we'll be on our way. Good evening to you." Yosef started to walk away.

"Wait." Crassus frowned angrily. "How did you escape?"

"I have *good* friends."

Crassus did not need to know that Gamliel, who routinely used Kaiaphas's key to visit prisoners in the dungeon cells, had secretly released him.

Yosef sucked in a halting breath and shifted his weight, waiting for the final hammer's fall.

The centurion said, "My orders are to arrest you for stealing the body of ben Pantera, and to return the body to the praefectus, but—"

"But we do not have the body. There is also no evidence that we are guilty of the theft of his body. Were you ordered to arrest us without evidence?"

If Pilatos had followed his own procedures, the body would have been the condemning evidence required to justify the arrest. Without it, the soldiers could not arrest him.

The centurion gazed at him with stony eyes. As night deepened, the horses began to wander into the shadows. Two of the soldiers went in search of them, and Yosef heard reins jingling as the men gathered the animals and led them back.

Upset, the centurion ordered, "We have no proof that any crime has been committed. Let's return to Jerusalem and report our findings to the praefectus."

A little resentfully, Yosef said, "Please give Lucius Pontios my regards."

The centurion glared at him, then waved his men forward. They mounted their horses and galloped up the twisting trail toward the main road. A gossamer haze of dust rose in their wake.

When they'd ridden out of sight, Yosef's legs failed him. He sat down hard. Titus kneeled in front of him, his eyes wide and filled with questions that Yosef did not know how to answer.

Yosef said, "The soldiers were waiting for you here?"

"Yes."

"How is that possible?"

Titus shifted uneasily. "I'm not sure. But...Master, on the way here, just outside of Emmaus, I passed two of the Rab's followers."[2]

"Which two?"

"Cleopas and Kepha."[3]

Yosef's gaze drifted over the dark orchard, the pack-horse tied to the tree, and the body on the ground. "Did you see them speaking with the Romans?"

"No, but why else would they be out here?"

Yosef concentrated on his heartbeat, which continued to slam against his ribs as though unaware that the danger had passed. "I don't know," he murmured. "This morning, Nisan the seventeenth, had been the first morning people were allowed to leave their homes. Maryam would have found the tomb empty and run to tell the disciples. Why weren't Kepha and Cleopas in Yerushalaim consoling their heartbroken, grieving flock, which numbered over one hundred people?

"Perhaps there was rioting and they needed to get away," he said.

Ioses didn't believe it.

Titus surveyed the darkness. "Where is the Dawn Bather? I didn't see you ride in with him."

"I left him a good distance back. I suspect that when he saw the soldiers, he assumed the worst. He and his brothers must have fled."

Titus's lips pressed together in disdain, as though he'd always known Mattias was a coward, but was restraining himself from voicing that opinion.

Yosef forced himself to breathe, hoping it would relieve some of his anxiety. His gaze returned to the body of Dysmas. The sense of utter astonishment had not diminished.

Bewildered, Titus said, "I don't understand. I thought we—"

"As did I."

Titus exhaled hard. "Well, now we have another problem. What shall we do with Dysmas? We can't just leave him out here for the wild animals."

"Let's bury him and be on our way."

"To where?"

Yosef ran a hand through his dirty hair. "Maryam wrapped the bodies in linen. She's the only one who knows the truth."

13

Following behind a young monk named Albion, Pappas Meridias tramped across the once beautiful city of Jerusalem. The boy was around fifteen years old, with soft brown eyes and short, sandy hair. His tattered brown robe looked as though it had recently been plucked from a trash heap. Meridias eyed it distastefully. Surely Pappas Macarios of Jerusalem could do better. Was he teaching the youth some lesson in poverty? Or perhaps self-denial? Regardless, such dress did not project the image of the Faith that Rome wished to cultivate. Who would convert if he thought he had to look like a derelict?

As they strode up the flagstone-paved street toward the hilltop, Meridias got a good view of the city. Remarkable. The devastation caused by the Tenth Legion during the Jewish Wars of 66 and 132 was still evident. The Temple Mount, at the emperor's orders, had been left in ruins, and everywhere he looked he saw the remains of Roman camps, as well as the infamous pagan temples built by Emperor Hadrian: the Temple honoring Jupiter built on the Temple Mount, and the Temple to Aphrodite built over the site of the crucifixion. From this angle, he could just see the top of Aphrodite's Temple.

After the defeat of Shimeon Bar Koseva and his rabble in 135, the Tenth Legion had remained in Jerusalem for almost two hundred years. Their main occupation had been the production of clay bricks baked in fireproof kilns. The demand for bricks was great, and each brick was marked with the Tenth Legion's emblem and trademark: LEG X.

As Meridias and the youth crested the hill and walked into a thick cloud of dust, Meridias drew a scarf from his pocket and placed it over his nose. Then he carefully scrutinized the huge excavation.[1]

Only the might of Rome could have orchestrated and engineered the filling and leveling of an entire valley. And now, only the might of Rome could have initiated the massive effort to restore an entire valley to its original condition.

Meridias might have stood atop some unnatural human hive. Hundreds of men carried baskets of dirt on their backs or shoveled it into carts to be hauled away. The mountains of refuse, stones, artifacts, and earth that had been dug up, were growing by the instant. As well, another group of laborers worked to tear down the magnificent Temple to Aphrodite. Meridias shook his head. In his opinion it was unfortunate that they couldn't have saved the structure and reconsecrated it to the Virgin Miriam, or to the Magdalen. But perhaps the emperor was right; it had been irreparably tainted by idolatry. Not only that, they had to remove the massive landfill if there was any hope of locating the actual remains of the crucifixion and tomb of Iesous. Unfortunately, the Temple to Aphrodite sat on part of the landfill.

"There he is," Albion said with a big, boyish smile. "Down there."

Meridias squinted against the dust and saw a man dressed in a long black robe apparently directing the excavation. He was short, with heavy jowls and wispy brown hair. "He's not very impressive, is he?" Meridias said.

Albion's smile dissolved in horror. "But he's a very holy man."

"Yes, well, perhaps he is. Let's go meet him."

Albion led the descent into the yawning excavation, picking his way through the gray haze. As they descended, the banging of hammers against chisels, of shovels striking hard-packed dirt and cart sides, along with the sharp ringing of picks on rocks, became almost unbearable.

Macarios saw him coming, detached himself from a group of engineers, and walked to meet Meridias with a smile on his ugly, dust-coated face. He had a large gap between his two front teeth.

"Pappas Meridias?" he greeted. "May the peace of our Lord be with you. I hope your arrival here has been—"

"Pappas Macarios," he interrupted with a dismal sigh. "I am happy to find you busy obeying the emperor's orders. What have you found?"

Macarios, clearly taken aback by the lack of polite opening conversation, said, "Uh, well, many things. Firstly, how was your journey?"

"Long and dirty. *What* have you found?"

Macarios blinked. "Well, to begin, let me explain that when Emperor Hadrian built the Temple to the god—"

"To the pagan deity Aphrodite," he corrected.

"Yes, of—of course. Anyway, in order to build the Temple, the emperor had to fill in the garden and the rocky escarpments to raise the level of the garden to the level of the remaining saddle of the mountain. We're talking tens of thousands of square cubits of—"

"I know all that. What have you found?"

Macarios's jowls jiggled as he rushed to say, "Just today we uncovered the rocky spur of Golgotha itself. That's it there." He pointed.

Through the dust, Meridias studied what looked like a small nondescript hump of rock. It was little more than a ridge of *malaky*, or royal stone. "What else?"

Macarios's expression drooped. "Well, on the west side, the escarpments of the saddle contain at least two tombs."

"Our Lord's tomb?"

"I don't know yet. Not for certain. We've only just begun our excavations. As we proceed, we will be able to answer your questions more reliably."

"That will be a welcome change. The emperor wants answers now."

Something on the ground caught his eye. Meridias reached down and pulled a small clay lamp from the soft earth. As he brushed it off, the image of a naked woman suspended with her legs spread over an erect male became clear. He roughly tossed it to the ground again.

Macarios glanced at it and said, "Appalling, aren't they? We've uncovered a number of pornographic oil lamps in the vicinity of the Tenth Legion's camps. Apparently they amused the soldiers."[2]

Meridias lifted his scarf and, again, covered his nose. Already his clean robe was coated with a fine powder, and he imagined that his blond hair looked the same.

Macarios studied his expression for several moments before bravely asking, "Meridias, can you tell me what this is all about? Pappas Silvester sent a series of questions regarding biblical place names that he wished me to answer. He seems to believe they are a map, but I could make no sense of them. Do you know what he's talking about?"

Gruffly, Meridias pulled a small roll of papyrus from his cape pocket. He'd written down every word he'd gleaned from the library assistants he'd questioned. He shoved it at Macarios. "Are these the names he sent you?"

Macarios took the papyrus and unrolled it. "Yes."

"I'm the one who provided Pappas Silvester with the list."

Macarios handed it back. "And where did you get it? It's very interesting, but I don't see how it could be important. We should focus—"

"That list has existed for almost three centuries, Macarios. I suspect it was written by Ioses of Arimathaia, at least that's what my sources suggest. It *is* important. Didn't you have any significant observations to report to Pappas Silvester after you reviewed it?"

Macarios flinched at his tone. For a time, he just stared at Meridias as though in a futile effort to peer past his eyes to locate a soul. Finally, he said, "I noted one thing."

"What was it?"

Macarios reached out gently and tapped a word in the middle of the papyrus. "This word intrigues me."

"*Selah*? What of it?"

"Well, the papyrus is written in Latin, but I wonder if the original Hebrew word wasn't really *Shelah,* from Nehemiah, chapter three, verse fifteen."

Irritated, Meridias demanded, "What difference would that make?"

Macarios drew himself to his full height and squared his shoulders. Apparently, knowledge had bolstered his courage. "A good deal, my brother. Since Shelah is located right there." He thrust his arm out, pointing to the south.

A strange, fiery sensation swelled around Meridias's heart. He took a step forward and tried to see what Macarios was pointing at. "I can't see anything through this haze. What's down there?"

"We call it the Pool of Siloam. Actually, there are two pools, an upper and a lower pool. They're fed by the Gihon Spring mentioned in First Kings, chapter one, verse thirty-three."

"What would it have to do with the word *Shelah*?"

"The pool has two names in the Hebrew holy books. In Isaiah it's called *Siloah,* but that same pool is referred to as *Shelah,* in Nehemiah. The terms also clearly referred to the area around the reservoirs as, for example, Luke says, in thirteen-four, that there was a tower in the place called 'the Siloam.'"

"So, you mean"—He paused while he considered the implications—"the entire area near the pools may have been called Siloam or Shelah?"

"Yes."

A gust of wind blew over the excavation and peppered Meridias's face with sand. He turned away until it passed, then stared in the direction of the pool again. "Why would the area around the pools have been important?"

Macarios opened his mouth to answer, but from behind Meridias, young Albion suggested, "Perhaps because of the tombs?"

"What tombs?" Meridias swung around to peer at the boy. He'd forgotten he was there. Albion was biting his lower lip as though expecting a reprimand for speaking up.

Albion looked to Macarios and softly said, "Forgive me, Pappas. I didn't mean to—"

"It's quite all right, Albion," Macarios said gently. "Go ahead and tell Pappas Meridias about the tombs."

As though excited, Albion broke into a silly grin. "They are everywhere, Pappas! The tombs fill every hole in the limestone, and we suspect there are many you can't even see because Emperor Hadrian covered over so many when he was filling the Kraniou Topon. But we—"

"Show me these tombs." Meridias took off without further discussion, striding down the hill toward the Siloam.

14

MELEKIEL—NISAN THE 14TH, THE TWELFTH HOUR OF DAY

I am standing in my home, sipping a cup of wine, surrounded by my four sisters and their families. The sun has set, but it is not yet Pesach. The Temple priests have not yet blown the horn to announce the arrival of the holy day. We are all waiting.

My eight nieces and nephews are running about, playing. But for the rest of us, this is a somber gathering. I couldn't bear to watch him die, to see the sacred light go out of his eyes, but as my sisters were preparing the Pesach meal, I watched the crucifixions from afar. Only Yeshua's female disciples were brave enough to follow him to the cross: Maryam, and Yeshua's two sisters, Mariam and Salome. They made certain that he did not die alone, but surrounded by people who loved him. They remained there, praying, through the entire terrible ordeal. It is perhaps curious that in Aramaic there is no feminine form of the word "disciple," talmida. but *through their deeds, Yeshua's female followers have proven themselves disciples nonetheless, especially in light of the fact that his male disciples betrayed, denied, and abandoned him.*

Shortly after the ninth hour, Centurion Petronius sent word that I could remove two of the bodies. Dysmas and Yeshua were dead. Gestas was still alive, still suffering.

A tremor goes through me. I only heard his voice once. At the end, he shouted, "My God, my God, why have you abandoned me?"[1] While the Romans in the crowd, who didn't understand Hebrew, began taunting him, saying that he was calling for Elijah to save him, I lifted my eyes to the heavens expecting to see a legion of angels descending, clothed in garments of pure light, or perhaps a pillar of fire, even a dove fluttering down to settle upon his head. A simple sign from God that he had not died in vain would have been enough.

I saw nothing but clear blue sky.[2]

I open my right palm and stare at it. I pulled out the nails myself, then lowered Yeshua's limp body into the arms of Titus, who carried him to the horse-drawn cart where he gently laid him down. Then we repeated the process with Dysmas. Because of the crowds of pagans and Greeks on the streets, it took almost an hour to get the bodies back here and placed in the newly hewn tomb in my garden.

Involuntarily, my eyes drift to the nails that rest in a pot upon my table. Nails removed from crucified victims are believed to have great medicinal value. They reduce swellings, inflammations, and fevers. Even the Romans hold that blood-soaked nails from victims of crucifixion cure epilepsy, and halt the spread of epidemics. Perhaps *that's why the only mode of crucifixion practiced by the Romans in Judea is crucifixion by nailing, not binding, the victim to the cross."[3] If I were wise, I would carry one of the nails with me, to protect me from illness...but I cannot bear to touch them. Besides, I have already made arrangements to return them to Pilatos in fulfillment of our agreement. He will count them carefully, and hold me to blame if one is missing.*

My gaze moves to the window where a charcoal veil is settling over the land. In my mind's eye, I imagine Maryam and Mariam in the tomb, preparing the bodies, annointing them with spices and oils, wrapping them in the finest linen I could afford.

"Yosef." My sister Yuan touches my sleeve. "The woman, Mariam, is at the door. She requests to speak with you. I told her you were grieving and that she should come back after the holy days, but she said it was urgent."

As though waking from a terrible nightmare, I blink at her pretty face, actually seeing it for the first time today, and say, "Thank you."

I stride past her, through the middle of my confused family, and duck out my doorway into the gray gleam of dusk. Mariam is standing quietly, wringing her hands. She is Yeshua's youngest sister, thirty-two, married to Clopas. They have two sons. The rest of her family is home celebrating, as best they can, the holy day. But she is here. She has her white himation pulled over her head and it accentuates the oval shape of her face and the size of her large, dark eyes. She looks very much like a female version of Yeshua.

"What is it, Mariam?"

"Forgive me for disturbing you, elder, but you must come. It—it's Maryam. I swear she has lost her mind!"

"What do you mean? What's happened?" I close the door behind me, blocking out the sounds of the sacred evening, of children's voices, and the smell of food. "Is she ill?"

When we arrived with the bodies at the tenth hour, we found Maryam standing by the tomb with a basket of spices. Her beautiful face had gone as pale as death. She hadn't wept, or railed. She'd just watched us carry the bodies into the tomb as though her soul had long ago left her body and flown away. Mariam arrived shortly there-after with an amphora of oil.

"Maryam asked me to go and fetch her himation. She'd left it near the cross today. She was getting cold. Even though I knew it was a long walk, I did it. It had been so hard to watch her, I actually welcomed the trip."

"Why was it hard to watch her?"

Tears fill her eyes. She uses the hem of her himation to wipe them. "For the longest time, she wouldn't let me near my brother's body. She was h-holding him, crying against his shoulder, sobbing, 'the light in the darkness shines, the light in the darkness shines.' She kept repeating those words. She wouldn't even let me wash the wounds in his hands and feet. Honestly, I didn't know what to do to comfort her."

"What happened when you returned with her himation?"

"She shouted at me to go away!" Mariam clutches Maryam's himation to her chest. "I called to her several times, but she told me to keep out or she'd kill me! When I tried to force my way in, she ran at me with a dagger! I *don't know where she got it, but her eyes blazed as though her demons had returned."*

"She's overwhelmed by grief, Mariam. That's all. I'm sure she isn't possessed—"

"You have to come and talk to her," she pleads and tugs at my sleeve. "She'll listen to you. She always has."

"I'll help any way I can."

I lead the way across the courtyard toward the tomb where faint lamplight etches a golden line around the stone that, when Maryam is finished preparing the dead, will be rolled over the entry to seal it until the holy days are over. Then we can finish preparing the bodies in our traditional ways.

Nearby, in the stable, lamplight also gleams. I try not to look at it, try not to draw Mariam's attention to it. I know Titus is in there saddling our horses, readying our packs. We will leave just after supper, after the city has quieted—but Mariam does not know this—nor does my family. Our conspiracy is small, consisting of only myself Maryam, two Essene brothers, and three of Yeshua's most trusted apostles. Even Titus does not know the whole truth, just the necessary facts.

The agonizing sound of muffled weeping reaches me long before I get to the tomb. She has always been brave. I am stricken to the heart by her cries. Not only that, the thought of arguing with a woman as grief-crazed as the one Mariam describes makes my soul shrivel. What can I do or say to ease her pain when my own is strangling me?

I stop by the stone outside, and call, "Maryam? It's Yosef. May I enter?"

The weeping stops. Sandals scrape the stone floor.

I stand irresolutely, wishing I could avoid this, then

I brace myself and call again, "Maryam, please let me see him. I need to see him."

She appears, and stares at me with wide, burning eyes. Insane eyes. Without a word, she grabs my hand and pulls me into the tomb. The two bodies are already wrapped in white linen, and the intoxicating fragrances of myrrh and aloe are almost staggering.

Maryam stands as though frozen, looking up at me with those wild eyes. "Yosef, please, I beg you. The savior himself must be saved. You understand that, don't you?"

I nod, endeavoring to appear calm. "That's what we're trying to do, Maryam. Tonight, we—"

"If you love them that love you, what reward have you?"

They are his words. I know, as well as she does, that Yeshua meant we must love our enemies. I stare into her strange eyes for a long moment. "Who are you talking about?"

She steps forward, very close to me, and whispers, "He would want us to save him, don't you see? And by saving him, we can save the savior."

I am totally confused now. "Maryam, please, slow down. I don't understand anything you're telling me. Yeshua would want us to save..."

Outside, down the lane, I hear hooves pounding. In only heartbeats, it becomes clear that the horses have turned onto the path to my home. Several men dismount.

"Yosef Haramati?" an authoritative voice calls.

"Here! I'm here." I hurry across the floor and duck outside into the dusk.

Four members of the Temple police stand holding their horses' reins. The captain of the guard says, "You are under arrest by the order of High Priest Kaiaphas."

Gamliel was right. They are deeply afraid. They mean to stop me.

All of my family rushes out of my house. My sisters begin shouting questions while my nieces and nephews bawl. My brothers-in-law tug their wives back as I am led away.

I mount the horse they've brought for me, and as we ride down the path toward the Damascus Gate, the horn blows. The sound echoes from the walls of the city and floods out over the surrounding hills.

The holy day has begun...it is Nisan the fifteenth.

15

Following behind Albion and Macarios, Meridias tramped by the beautiful rocked-in Pool of Siloam with its intricate mosaic floor, and out of the city through the Dung Gate.

Macarios extended his hand to the steep valley that dropped away in front of them. In the late afternoon light, the upthrust rocks and brush cast long, dark shadows over the limestone slopes now tawny with sparse grasses. What he could see of the far slope was dotted with small black holes, some in flats carved from the valley stone. Faint trails crisscrossed the slope as though woven between the features.

Macarios spoke reverently. "This is the Hinnom valley."

Meridias studied the narrow gorge. The length of it curved along the west and south sides of Jerusalem like a V-shaped moat. "What is the name of the valley that the gorge intersects at the bottom?"

"The Kidron valley."

Both the Hinnom and Kidron valleys were areas of

exposed limestone ridges and wind-smoothed barren hillocks. If there ever had been any trees here, they'd all been cut down and used by the soldiers of the Tenth Legion to warm themselves, cook their food, and bake their bricks. Now only scrub brush and grass filled the spaces between the rocks.

"Here, Pappas, let me show you some of the most interesting tombs," Albion said and started off down the slope at a fast walk.

Meridias, careful of the footing, fell into line behind him. As they made their way along the precarious trail, he noted the numerous fragments of incised limestone slabs that had been scattered down the slope. Some of the stonework was extraordinary. "Macarios? What are these?"

Macarios strode up beside him and looked at where Meridias pointed. "I'm afraid those are pieces of broken ossuaries, bone boxes. Grave robbers always come out after dark to plunder the tombs."

"Grave robbers?"

"Yes, we post guards, of course, but it does little good. We don't have enough people. They raid the tombs looking for precious jewels, gold, anything they can sell."

"They break into the tombs and drag out the ossuaries?"

"Or crush them inside the tombs. But I suppose it's easier to see the contents if you drag the ossuaries outside into the light."

The path down curved into a gorge where the walls of limestone rose three or four times their height. They passed several rock-hewn tombs with rectangular and T-shaped doorways blocked by stones.

"How old are these ossuaries?" Meridias asked.

"Ossuaries were used for burials for only a very short time—we suspect from about thirty years before the birth of our Lord, until the destruction of the Temple in the year seventy."

"So they date to the time of our Lord?"

"Approximately, yes."

Albion called, "Here! Pappas Meridias, come and look at this one!"

Meridias hurried to the place where the youth stood. The tomb facade was magnificent. The stoneworker had hacked a man-sized square at least three fathoms back into the face of the limestone wall, flattened it, and cut a T-shaped doorway, which had been sealed with a stone. Above the doorway, three elaborate interconnected circles had been carved. Each circle had an incised border of triangles, and what appeared to be a large six-petaled flower in the middle.

Meridias said, "It's beautiful. I had no idea the Ioudaiosoi were such skilled stoneworkers."

Albion smiled, pleased by his response. "This is my favorite, but there are thousands of tombs here. Would you like to see more of the special ones?"

"No. Not today. I'm tired. But perhaps tomorrow."

Albion said, "Yes, Pappas."

Macarios gave Albion a proud nod. "Thank you, brother, for your help today. Can you take Pappas Meridias back to the cell we prepared for him in the monastery?"

"Of course. Please follow me."

Albion started back up the gorge trail and Meridias followed close behind Macarios. The sun had set, and dusk was descending over the city.

The climb was strenuous. They were both breathing hard when they climbed out of the gorge and started up the slope for the city.

Meridias stopped to catch his breath. While Albion continued up the hill, he turned to Macarios. "Tomorrow, first thing, I want to see the two tombs you found near Golgotha."

Macarios used his sleeve to wipe the sweat from his jowls and nodded. "Of course. Our workers should have more cleared by then. Perhaps we will be able—"

"Pappas Macarios!" Albion cried.

Macarios jerked his head up, strode past Meridias, and climbed the rocky slope toward the young monk who was standing bent over with his hands propped on his knees.

As Meridias followed in Macarios's footsteps, he saw the soft dirt pile before the freshly opened tomb. Broken fragments of ossuaries littered the ground in front, and he could clearly see the doorway, measuring about one fathom square.

Macarios kneeled and peered into the tomb, as though hoping to find one of the grave robbers still at work so he could arrest them.

Meridias stood a few paces back. "Do you see anyone?"

"No, but it's very dark in there...and the tomb is larger than I would have thought given its unimpressive facade."

Meridias went to kneel beside Macarios and look inside. A damp, musty scent breathed from the tomb, which sent a chill up Meridias's spine. "Let's see what's in there."

"You're going in?" Macarios asked in surprise.

"What if the thieves are hiding in one of the inner chambers?"

"Surely we scared them away," he answered as he got on his hands and knees and crawled into the darkness.

Once through the opening, the tomb yawned around him, soaring twice his height and spreading ten fathoms across. Despite his brave words, Meridias reached for the long-bladed dagger he kept under his robes. Stairs led downward. He took them one at a time, dagger ready, fingertips tracing the close wall on his left. In ten heartbeats his eyes began to adjust and objects crystallized. There were at least twenty ossuaries resting on stone shelves. He called up, "It's safe. You can enter."

Macarios and Albion crawled in and climbed down the steps. As their eyes adjusted, Meridias walked to the stone shelf on the left, where two ossuaries nestled side by side. There were words written on them. He could see them in the faint light that penetrated through the doorway.

"Macarios, when you can see, come over here. You read Hebrew, don't you?"

"Yes." Macarios walked toward him, blinking his eyes.

Albion stood as though frozen to the floor, looking around wide-eyed.

Macarios bent to study the words scratched into the ossuaries. "Hmm. This one says *Salome.*"

Meridias dusted off the word on the other ossuary. "And this one?"

Macarios squinted at it. "It's not very clear, but it may be *Mari,* or *Mariam.*"

Albion sucked in a sudden breath. His eyes had adjusted, and he lifted a shaking arm to point at something in the rear of the tomb. "It—it's a skeleton!"

"Where?" Meridias spun around to look.

"Back there, lying on that rock shelf."

Meridias edged around the broken chunks of ossuaries that had been destroyed by the thieves in their haste, and made his way toward the rear. "Dear God, Albion's right."

A skeleton lay on its back, a burial shroud covering the collapsed ribs, arms, and legs. The fabric had been drawn back to expose the skull. It gleamed as though sculpted of polished brown marble."[1]

Macarios came up beside him. "I wonder why his bones were never collected and placed in an ossuary as was customary."

"His family must have brought him here, sealed the tomb, and never returned to finish the work," Meridias suggested. "Maybe he was one of the last ones, left behind when the Temple was destroyed?"

"That's possible. According to the ancient texts, a corpse was prepared with oil and spices, then wrapped in white linen and placed on a shelf in a tomb. After which, the tomb was closed up with a blocking stone. In a year or so, the stone was rolled aside and the bones of the dead were collected and placed in a box, usually made of limestone—though those in the Galilaian seem to have been made of clay."

"Why didn't they just bury them and be done with it?" Meridias asked.

"Some people did, but the Pharisees believed—as we do—in the physical resurrection of the body. The decomposition of the flesh supposedly cleansed the body of sin and left the bones in a pure state, ready for the resurrection."

"Then the tradition of ossuaries was strictly a Pharisaic one?"

"I believe it was primarily practiced by the Pharisees, but that's all I can say."

Meridias cautiously walked toward the skeleton. As he neared the shelf, he noticed a darker patch to his left, and could make out at least two steps. "There's another chamber," he said. "It looks like it goes down to a lower level."

Albion's young voice had gone shrill with fear. "We n-need a torch or a lamp. Perhaps we should return tomorrow with the proper equipment to search the rest of the tomb."

"I agree. It's getting dark outside," Macarios said. "When we return to the monastery, I'll dispatch monks to guard this tomb until we can reseal it."

"Reseal it?" Meridias said.

"Well, yes. Out of respect for the dead, we should—"

"We should probably reseat the blocking stone, and then bury it beneath as much earth as we can," Meridias said, "or the thieves will certainly return."

Macarios tilted his head in reluctant agreement. "That is a good suggestion, brother. I'll pull some workers off our excavation and send them over here in the morning."

Macarios and Albion climbed up the stairs and when their bodies blocked the light, the tomb went utterly black. Meridias stood with his eyes focused on the place where he knew the shrouded skeleton rested. A strange prickling crept up his spine. He sensed or heard something. *Probably the wind outside.* It grew louder, and sounded oddly like a soft, mournful voice. In mere moments it seemed to fill the chamber.

Meridias backed toward the steps. A fear like nothing he had ever known rose inside him. He was certain now that it was a man's voice.

Finally, both Albion and Macarios crawled out, and light once again streamed into the chamber.

The sound vanished.

Meridias forced a deep breath into his lungs. With the light restored, the tomb was, once again, utterly quiet.

"Are you coining, Pappas Meridias?" Macarios called.

"Yes."

As he made his way out into the dusk, he silently cursed himself for being a fool and strode bravely for the city gate.

16

Loukas sat his horse atop a hill; his remaining men slouched on their mounts just behind him. On the road below, Atinius, the woman, and the other two monks made their way toward Jerusalem. His eyes focused on the woman.

I'm coming for you.

"Why are we waiting?" Elicius asked. "They're too far ahead. We should be going."

"In a moment," Loukas answered without looking at the old man.

The Holy City draped like a cluttered blanket over a rounded mountaintop. In the distance the massive stone walls gleamed faintly blue with the falling of night. Broken in many places by former sieges, the wall was no longer a defensive structure. Rather, it had become an ancient artifact of toppled stones, interspersed with remnants of standing walls—more a monument to Roman superiority than to the engineering skills of the Ioudaiosoi.

Just outside the Damascus Gate, Loukas could see

the massive, partially completed monastery. Meridias should be there. Was he watching, even as Atinius and his companions rode past?

"I thought they would have headed for Apollonia, or perhaps Caesarea. I'm stunned that they came here," Elicius said with a shake of his gray head. "Pappas Meridias was right about spooking them."

The old man had a doglike face with a long snout and fierce brown eyes. After a week on the trail his once-shaven face had again sprouted gray hair. It covered his cheeks and chin, making him seem old beyond belief. Alexander, the second men, sat his horse a few paces away, silent.

Loukas kept his eyes on the prey. Atinius had almost reached the northern gate that led into the city, the Damascus Gate. As part of his training, the Militia Templi had required that he study the Holy City. After the death of Iesous Christos, it had been transformed from an earthly city into a celestial one: the heavenly Jerusalem. His gaze took in the legendary Temple Mount and the ruins of what had once been the most extraordinary sacred space on earth, then drifted to the still standing towers of the Citadel to the west, which had served as the royal palace of King Herod. He could see the vast excavation ordered by Emperor Constantine, and the dust pall that trailed off to the east, carried by the breeze.

Jerusalem! Reverence filled him. He was a soldier of the Faith, sworn to protect it, and this place, this broken city, was its heart. Whatever monstrous thing Atinius and his allies were after, he had to stop them from finding it. Or if they did, he was bound to destroy it before anyone knew it had existed.

Loukas remained, squinting in the darkness as Atinius finally passed through the gate, followed by the other horse and riders.

"Are you sure we can find them in there?" Elicius asked.

"Quite sure." Loukas kicked his horse into a trot and continued his pursuit.

As night deepened, the scent of tilled soil wafted on the breeze, along with the musky odor of animal dung. Tawdry little huts dotted the hillsides leading to the Holy City, and he could make out corrals filled with one or two cows, maybe a few sheep or goats. As they passed, hidden horses, lodged in barns, whinnied and their own horses pranced and answered.

Just before they began the final steep climb to the city, Elicius rode up beside him. "Should we find Pappas Meridias and report before we continue our pursuit?"

Loukas gave him a withering look. "We stick as close to our prey as possible. Meridias can wait."

17

Barnabas guided his horse beneath the massive gray stone arch of the Damascus Gate. Despite his exhaustion and fear, he felt Jerusalem's influence as powerfully now as he had when he'd first visited here thirty years ago. The air was cool and still between the tumbled walls, and a divine loneliness seemed to seep from the very earth itself, as though the city grieved a loss that human beings would never be able to comprehend. Even in the growing darkness, he could make out the ruins on the Temple Mount and the dust rising from the massive excavation they'd noticed as they'd ridden in. The slight breeze had stretched the haze over the city like a gauzy burial shroud, accentuating the smell of ancient destruction.

Cyrus straightened. He raised an arm to point. "Is that the Square of the Column?"

"Yes," Barnabas replied.

As they rode forward, lamps glittered to life behind the small windows. People passed, most dressed in white robes. The smells of evening fires, burning oil, old urine, and cooking food carried on the air.

Barnabas reined his horse to a stop at the base of the Square of the Column. Tall and round, it stood in the middle of a central plaza where the streets branched. Upper Market Street ran off to his right and Lower Market Street to his left.

For a time, Barnabas just stared at the column. He was vaguely aware that Cyrus had tilted his head back to stare up at the square cap on top of the column.

Yes, this is the place. If a man studied it carefully, he could see the symbol of the *tekton*. He had only to turn it into a two-dimensional figure. Cut that square base in half and it appeared to be an inverted *V* tented over a circle: the round column.

Kalay asked, "Which street are we taking?"

"Lower Market Street. We're heading for the Temple Mount. There are a number of pools and fountains there."

Barnabas's horse lifted its nose, sniffed the air, and let out a low whinny, as though scenting other horses, or perhaps a barn with fresh hay. The poor animals were hungry after the past two days when they'd only been able to nibble grass along the road.

As they plodded up the flagstoned street, the painfully sweet strains of reed pipes rose and fell, eddying on the wind. Someone was baking bread, and the smell of boiling spelt sent a quiver through Barnabas's empty stomach.

They passed four monks in brown robes walking back toward the gate. Their hoods were up, so Barnabas never saw their faces, but the monk who walked in front called, "May the Lord's peace be with you."

"And with you, brothers," Barnabas, Cyrus, and Zarathan answered in unison.

They'd ridden by what appeared to be a monastery being constructed north of the Damascus Gate. Perhaps that's the place these monks were headed.

Flat-topped homes crowded together on both sides of the road, their shared gardens adorned by palm and fig trees that swayed in the night breeze.

Several people were still out, walking up and down the street. Barnabas and his friends received quick glances, but little more.

As they continued south, the majesty of the Temple Mount became apparent. The stone retaining walls that supported the Temple platform were still mostly intact and stood eight to ten times the height of a man.

"I've always thought it must have been unbelievable before the revolt in the year 66," Cyrus said in awe.

"It was." Kalay gazed up at the top of the Western Wall and the few stars visible beyond. "The Temple was covered with gold. You could see it shining, like a beacon, from a half day's walk away."

"Yes, it was one of the great wonders of the world, and the house where God's presence resided," Barnabas added. In his mind he could see the massive arches and endless rows of columns, the vaulted ceilings, underground passageways, and ingenious aqueducts—all the things he'd seen or read about. "I suspect no other building in the world has heard as many prayers, or seen as many pilgrimages. Or, perhaps, witnessed as much suffering."

As they neared the Beautiful Gate, Barnabas said, "There's a pool just inside where we can water our horses."

"Yes," Kalay said. "I remember that from when I was here before."

"As do I." Cyrus led his horse through the gate and stopped, his eyes warily on the empty street behind them, as if expecting to see furtive movement. Kalay slid off and winced.

"You may dismount, brother," Barnabas said, aware that Zarathan was staring unabashedly at Kalay as she arched her tired back and her dress pulled tight across her chest.

Zarathan jumped down and stood awkwardly, his gaze darting from one shadow to the next, trying to look in any direction that wasn't toward Kalay. "What are we doing here? Why couldn't we have asked for food and lodging at the monastery outside the city? That's what that was, wasn't it? A monastery?"

"I wasn't sure, brother. I thought it better not to take chances."

Barnabas dismounted, took the reins, and led his horse to the rocked-in pool. Their horse was sucking up water as fast as it could, long swallows running up its neck like mice. Barnabas sat wearily on the edge of the pool while his horse drank, and heaved a heavy sigh. He could feel every muscle in his body. His bones might have been stone, so heavy did they feel.

Have I ever been this fatigued?

Narrow streets radiated off from this plaza, but to the east, a broad stone staircase led up to the top of the Temple Mount. The last time he was here, the ruins were little more than massive piles of stones too big to be carted off. Over the centuries, everything that could be taken and sold had been. But not the largest stones.

They remained as mute testaments to the extraordinary engineers who'd cut and laid them.

"We're going up to the ruins of the Temple?" Kalay asked between dipping handfuls of water and drinking them.

"Yes."

She dried her fingers on her dirty tan dress. "Why?"

Hesitantly, he answered, "I need to test one of Libni's hypotheses, but please don't ask me to explain it. It's farfetched."

Kalay exchanged a concerned glance with Cyrus, who said, "I'm willing to help you test whatever you wish, brother; but let us be quick about it. This place stinks of a trap."

Zarathan eagerly added, "For once, I agree. I think the only safe place is the monastery just outside the city. We should go back there and ask for lodging and food."

"You're an imbecile. That monastery is about as safe as your monastery in Egypt was," Kalay said.

Zarathan glowered at her. "You have a poison tongue. Do you know that?"

"At least mine is still in my head. I'm afraid yours is going to end up ripped out of your mouth by one of Meridias's fanatical followers and left lying on a table."

The full moon edged above the Mount and sent a pale flood over the sky. The horses temporarily stopped drinking to look up, then lowered their heads again.

"Why would someone torture me?" Zarathan asked. "I don't know anything."

"The problem is they don't know you're completely ignorant. They probably think you've read a papyrus or two. Even *the* papyrus. And once they find out you have read it they have ways to make sure you never tell anyone about it." She stuck out her tongue and made a sawing motion with her finger.

Zarathan winced and drew back.

Barnabas tugged his horse toward the hitching rail that abutted one of the dark walls near the Beautiful Gate. "Brother," Barnabas said to Zarathan as he tied his horse to it. "Could you help me lift the book bags down?"

"Why?" Zarathan demanded as though greatly aggrieved by the request. "You're not planning on hauling those around with us all night, are you? Why don't we leave them here? I'll be happy to stay with the horses and guard them."

Cyrus said, "No. We stay together." He tied his horse to the rail and shouldered past Zarathan to get to Barnabas. Together, they lifted the precious bags off and gently rested them on the ground.

"But I want to stay with the horses!" Zarathan pleaded with such persistence that Barnabas wondered if he might be planning on taking one and riding back to the monastery in search of food.

Cyrus ominously said, "It's too dangerous, brother. This is Jerusalem. From now on, we should never be out of each other's sight."

Zarathan's face twisted into a pout. "But where are we going to sleep? I'm tired!"

As Barnabas separated the two bags, untying them to make them easier to carry, he said, "We'll decide after we've finished our task on the Temple Mount."

Kalay started off in that direction, and Cyrus said, "Brothers, go ahead of me. I'll bring up the rear."

"Thank you, Cyrus."

Barnabas and Zarathan each picked up a book bag and marched after Kalay. As they climbed the stairs, Zarathan started making small, tormented sounds, as though the weight of the bag was far too much for him to carry—or at least for him to carry on an empty stomach. Barnabas decided not to ask; he knew the answer.

At the top of the stairs, they stepped out onto the paved Temple grounds and Barnabas took a few moments to catch his breath.

The sound of Cyrus's footsteps coming up behind him had a feline quality, soft and deliberate, as though stalking an unsuspecting bird.

"Where do we go from here?" Cyrus murmured.

Barnabas turned. "The Western Wall. It has a good view. Follow me."

18

Loukas crouched in a shadowed alleyway, gazing up at the Temple Mount and the three people high above who clustered at the edge of the massive retaining wall. In the moonlight, they appeared as black silhouettes. What perfect targets they made for a good archer. It surprised him that Atinius would make such a careless error.

"What are they doing?" Elicius asked from two paces away, where he and Alexander—their gray heads shimmering in the silver light—held the reins of their horses.

Loukas answered, "Just standing there."

"They seem to be looking out at the city," Alexander said. "Why?"

"I don't know."

"The Temple Mount makes a perfect trap. Perhaps we should go up after them?"

Loukas slowly shook his head. He couldn't afford any extravagant motions. Despite their shadowed location, he wasn't certain that they were totally concealed from Atinius's view. "No."

"Why not?" Elicius challenged. "It would be easy to corner them up there."

Alexander added. "We could force them to tell us what they know."

It amazed him that Pappas Athanasios had relied upon and trusted men like Elicius and Alexander. Did Loukas truly have to explain that it was wiser and less time-consuming to let the prey lead them to the "monstrous thing"? Perhaps in their youth these old men had been great soldiers of the Faith, but if so, age had simply dulled their wits.

Or did Pappas Athanasios foist them off on me with the expectation that they'd fail? Perhaps he wants them dead as much as I do.

Loukas said, "Stop asking me ridiculous questions. I don't have the time to keep answering them."

Elicius's eyes narrowed in anger. The old man was accustomed to giving orders, not receiving them. Having to obey Loukas clearly irked him.

"Do you have a plan? I don't think that's a ridiculous question."

Softly, Loukas replied, "We wait for them to move, then we follow from a respectable distance. That's the plan. Do you understand?"

"Of course I understand."

"And you, Alexander? Do you understand?"

The old man gave him a hateful glare. But nodded.

19

Cyrus's sword belt jangled as he walked forward, calling, "Brother Barnabas, it's not a good idea to stand at the wall. You're clearly visible from below. If someone wishes—"

"I won't be long, Cyrus. Please give me just a few more moments."

Cyrus stood behind his three friends, watching as they gathered around the papyrus that Barnabas had spread out on the stone wall.

He clenched his jaw, worried.

Cyrus knew—as perhaps none of them did—that they had almost certainly been followed. The man who'd fled the fight at Libni's cave would have reported to his superiors. There weren't that many roads to watch, and three priests and a striking red-haired woman on two horses would be easily spotted. That no one had tried to ambush them on the road meant Meridias and his agents knew where they were headed. Perhaps they had decided it was smarter to allow Barnabas to find the Pearl and simply take it.

Not only that, Cyrus could *feel* eyes upon them, watching them.

He looked back at Barnabas. From up here, they had a clear view of the city that sprawled over the hills in every direction, and Barnabas seemed to be comparing the papyrus to Jerusalem.

Cyrus once again scanned the Temple Mount with its massive toppled stones, then his eyes drifted to the street far below that ran due east–west. So bright was the moonlight that he could trace the patterns in the flagstones, see the rosette designs that decorated the doors of houses, and discern even the shadows of fallen palm fronds. There were many people outside, some sitting in their gardens, others walking the streets. In the distance, Upper Market Street gleamed brilliantly silver in contrast to the gaping black hole of the excavation.

The Temple to Aphrodite was half torn down, its foundations about to be devoured by the pit. He wondered what they were looking for. The site of the crucifixion? Perhaps the tomb of Iesous?

Kalay said something soft to Barnabas that he couldn't hear and tapped the map. Though she'd braided her long red hair, the wind had pried several tendrils loose and draped them in damp ringlets across her forehead and cheeks. She looked achingly beautiful.

Perhaps, when this was all over—no. Not even then.

He'd made his choice years ago. He'd given his sacred vows, promised his soul to his Lord. But as he watched her, he felt a desperate longing. No matter what he tried to tell himself, his attraction for this woman was turning to love. And he seemed incapable of stopping the metamorphosis.

When she glanced up and noticed his gaze, she gave

him a small smile, and a discouraging shake of the head, as though she'd understood his heart at once.

He spread his feet and forced himself to watch the city.

Finally Barnabas called, "Cyrus, could you come and examine this?"

He walked forward and looked at the papyrus held down by Barnabas's dirty fingers. "What am I looking for?"

"Anything. Libni thinks the cross symbol at the bottom of the papyrus may designate roads. Do you see any resemblance between the symbol and the roads visible in front of us?"

Cyrus bent to examine the symbol. Despite the moonlight, it wasn't easy to see. The smoky scent of Barnabas's clothing mingled with the unmistakable odors of unwashed bodies and horse sweat. Oddly, he found them comforting, for it reminded him of long-ago military camps, of battles won and the smiles of long-lost friends.

Cyrus gazed northward. "The V at the top of the symbol is similar to the branching of Upper and Lower Market streets at the Damascus Gate. After that...there are too many hills and houses to be able to see the streets...even from up here."

"Yes, but Lower Market Street," Kalay said with her finger hovering over the long right arm of the symbol, "really does look like it matches this part of the symbol."

"And the far north–south line, though we can't trace it out fully, seems to match Upper Market Street," Barnabas said.

"Well"—Cyrus made an airy gesture with his hand

—"then I think the street below us, that runs east–west, may match the crossbar of the symbol."

Zarathan's stomach growled loudly. Irritably, he said, "Oh, this is ludicrous. Watch, I can play the game, too. Do you see the small crosses on the map? I'm sure they match those crude stone walls you can see over there, and over there, and over there. And if the long right arm on the papyrus is Lower Market Street, it runs right down into that valley to the south. So who wants to go with me and see if we find buried treasure?" He made a deep-throated sound of disgust. "This is all just useless. You can make anything out of the crosses. We should leave and go beg for—"

Barnabas's sharp gasp silenced everyone.

With trembling hands, he lifted the papyrus and his fingertip touched the small crosses on the papyrus one by one before pointing in turn toward the stone walls Zarathan had indicated. After several moments, a tiny, pitiful cry escaped his throat. "Blessed God."

"What is it?" Cyrus asked. "What do you see?"

Tears streamed down Barnabas's face as he stared unblinking at Jerusalem.

"Brother!" Zarathan said. "Forgive me. I didn't mean to upset you. I was just being frivolous."

Kalay pulled the map from Barnabas's hands and repeated his actions, glancing down at the small crosses, then up to the distant stone walls. It seemed an eternity before she said, "When I came here as a child, I remember those stone walls enclosed Roman camps." She extended her arm to point out each one. "To the south was the Temple Mount camp. To the southwest, the Mount Zion camp, and due west was the Palace camp. Why would someone hundreds of years ago have used crosses to mark Roman camps?"

Though absolutely silent, Barnabas was sobbing uncontrollably.

Cyrus took the papyrus from Kalay's hand. He, too, had made a pilgrimage here when those stone walls had been filled with Roman soldiers. He remembered the colorful flags flying over the gates and the—

It hit him like a blunt beam in the stomach. He straightened. As full understanding dawned, it seemed to hollow out his insides, leaving behind a black, empty husk that throbbed.

"Do you see it?" Barnabas wept the words and turned to look up at Cyrus with tear-drenched cheeks.

"Oh, yes," he whispered. "They're not crosses."

Surprised, Zarathan frowned. "They're not? Then what are they?"

Cyrus's gaze fixed on the road that led south into the night-silvered Kidron valley, and quietly answered, "Roman numerals. Tens. For the Tenth Legion. We're standing in the middle of the map."

20

NISAN THE 18TH, MIDNIGHT

I expected to see a city in the grips of rioting with half the buildings on fire, or perhaps the aftermath of forced suppression with precious belongings strewn, dead bodies lining the streets, and Roman legions crawling all over.

But an eerie quiet possesses Yerushalaim.

The city looks iron gray in the cold grip of night. We trot our horses through the endless wheat and barley fields that encircle the north side of the city and head east toward Bet Ani.

"It's too quiet," Titus whispers from where he rides to my right.

"I know."

"Perhaps the praefectus ordered a curfew."

"Perhaps, but if so, where are the soldiers to enforce it? I count barely a handful of men standing guard in front of the gate east of the Temple Mount."

Titus swivels on his horse to look and frowns. "Where are the other soldiers?"

"Somewhere else."

"Master...listen. There are no babies crying, no dogs barking. Not even any drunken laughter. It's as though..."

He doesn't finish, and I don't have the courage to do it for him.

It's as though the world has died.

We ride on into the queer leaden light that swaths the fields and the trees that grow on the west side of the Mount of Olives. Was it so long ago that I found Yeshua at the foot of the Mount after he had thrown the merchants from the Temple porches?

Wrenching sadness knots my belly. I inhale the faint green fragrance of recently sprouted wheat. I desperately wish I could go back...

"What if Maryam isn't there, Master?"

"Her family will know where she is."

"She was the Rab's constant companion. She may have been arrested."

"If she was arrested by the Council, they just questioned her and let her go. If she was questioned by the praefectus's skilled interrogators, she told them everything...and you and I are both as good as dead."

Titus shifts on his horse and looks straight ahead again, paying attention to the road.

"Titus, if we don't find her tonight, I promise we'll ride on. We'll get as far away from here as we can."

We turn down the street where Maryam's family has lived for generations. Our horses' hooves slip and skid on the cobblestones as we make our way down the row of flat-topped houses and alongside the beautiful gardens *filled with fig and date trees. No lamps burn in any of the houses. It is a strange, unearthly sight.*

"Stay here," I order and give my reins to Titus to hold. "Be ready to run."

"Yes, Master."

I sprint up the steps to her father's door and knock, lightly at first, then, when no one comes, harder.

Voices hiss inside, asking questions. A single lamp is lit. Through the windows, I see its wavering light moving.

A man opens the door a slit and peers out. When recognition dawns, he flings the door wide open. "Yosef Haramati!" Lazaros, Maryam's brother, cries. "Come in. Quickly!"

I step inside and he closes the door.

"They're looking for you. Do you know that? Everyone is looking for you. The Council, the praefectus, the multitudes—"

"Yes, yes, I know," I say. "Forgive me for endangering your family by coming here, but I must speak with Maryam. Is she here?"

The scent of roasted goat fills the house. It is a large, lovely place, with gorgeous rugs on the floors and many scrolls on shelves. It is too dark to see much else. The small lamp flame is barely enough to allow me to clearly see Lazaros's round face. He is tall and thin, with brown hair and a beard. His dark eyes are wide, as though he's just suffered a fright.

"No, she's not here, she..." Lazaros stops as though stunned. "You haven't heard?"

"Heard what?"

He stares at me dumbly for several heartbeats. "The Rab...he's risen."

"Risen?"

Excitedly, he says, "Yes! This morning, Maryam and the other women went to the tomb and found it empty! The Rab was gone. It's a miracle!" Tears blur his eyes. His voice grows soft and reverent. "Just as the prophecies foretold, elder! He rose and ascended to sit at the right hand of God."

I stammer, "L-Lazaros, what happened this morning when people could first leave their homes? Did the Zealots—"

"Oh, elder, it was terrifying. The Zealots had gathered five thousand strong to remove the body of Gestas from the cross. He'd died sometime over the holy days, no one knows when. The Zealots were angry, stamping around, whipping up hatred, accusing Rome of murdering three sons of Yisrael—"

"What of Pilatos? What did he do?"

"He dispatched three Roman legions to surround the Zealots. I heard that they had orders to slaughter everyone—man, woman, and child—at the slightest provocation. You could feel the fear in the air." He paused and turned glowing eyes on Yosef.

"But?"

"Before dawn, right after she'd visited the tomb, Maryam ordered the women to run in different directions proclaiming the startling news. She herself went to the disciples. Kepha...Kepha told her he didn't believe her.[1] But she didn't stop, she ran to the Zealots. In less than three hours, Maryam and the other women had told everyone that the Rab had risen. I swear the story spread like wildfire."

"And the Zealots?"

"It was like a flood, a human flood. Thousands of the

Zealots ran to your home to see the tomb. Every person wanted to touch the cast-off burial cloths. I think the entire city of Yerushalaim is empty tonight because people are still camped all over the hills around your house, waiting their turns."

I am thinking only, Gamliel...thank you, God, for Gamliel.

"One other thing, elder," Lazaros says.

"Yes?"

"There was a man dressed in white in the tomb. He told Maryam that the Rab had given him a message to deliver. He said that the Rab would meet his disciples and Kepha in the Galil."

"His disciples and Kepha? Meaning Kepha is no longer one of his disciples?"

Lazaros shrugs uncertainly. "I don't know, the man didn't—"

"Do you have any idea where Maryam might be? I must speak with her."

Lazaros gestures lamely. "Elder, we haven't seen Maryam since before the crucifixions. She sent Yoanna to tell us about the miracle. But I did hear a rumor that someone had seen her in the Kidron valley just after sunset. I don't know why she would be down there when she could come home, but—"

"Thank you," I say and bow. My heart has begun to thunder. "I'll be on my way now. The less time I spend here, the safer you and your family will be." I turn and swiftly walk for the door.

Lazaros rushes ahead to pull it open for me. "Elder, please be careful. If the crowds recognize you, the soldiers—"

"Yes, I know. I will."

Without a goodbye, I step out the door and run for my horse. Titus, probably fearing we've been discovered, kicks our horses around and holds my reins out for me to grab.

I take them, mount my horse, and we ride away down the street at a gallop.

"What's wrong?" Titus asks. "Was Maryam there?"

"No." I shake my head. "But I think I know where she is."

21

The wind picked up the instant they stepped outside the Dung Gate. Zarathan grimaced as another gust whipped his long robe into snapping folds and hurled gravel at his eyes. He squinted in defense.

Three paces ahead of him, Cyrus and Barnabas led the horses down the steep trail, apparently unaffected by the gale. He didn't know where Kalay was, probably out in front of the horses or he'd be able to see her.

He started walking again.

In the moonlight, the slope seemed to be littered with massive misshapen beasts, though when he walked up to them they turned out to be limestone outcrops. He sidestepped another one, and plodded onward with his head down.

For over two hours, they'd been examining one squat, ugly tomb after another, and found nothing interesting.

The horses stopped ahead of him, and Cyrus said,

"This path is too steep to take our horses down. We'll have to go the rest of the way on foot."

Barnabas stared at the deep, moonlit gorge, then turned to look back at the Dung Gate, tracing out a straight line like the one shown on the papyrus. "Yes, you're right. We don't have the luxury of going around or we may lose our bearings. Let's find a rock or bush to tie our horses to."

Zarathan walked forward and gazed down into the gorge. In the bottom, a narrow, winding path led south into the Kidron valley.

As Cyrus and Barnabas hunted for a good place to tie the horses, Zarathan stood in the background with his arms folded, moping.

Kalay's mouth quirked when she saw him. She walked over and said, "You look like you ate a horse apple."

"As you well know, I haven't eaten anything for two days, let alone a horse apple."

"Why don't you try to be helpful and find a rock to tie the horses to? It will make you forget your hunger, and"—she stressed the words—"would be good for your soul."

Tartly, he replied, "How would you know? You're an unchaste, pagan demon-worshipper."

Kalay propped her hands on her hips. "I've been demoted to just a demon-worshipper? I liked it better when I was a full demon." She gave him an evil look, hitched up her dress, and tramped away after Cyrus and Barnabas.

Zarathan took a quick look around and rapidly followed her. The last thing he wanted was to be left alone out here.

Just after they'd exited the Dung Gate, Barnabas had wanted to turn right, to follow the short leg of the map that branched off to the west of the long straight leg, but they'd seen two men standing in that direction, and decided it would be best to follow out the long leg instead.

"This will do," Barnabas said.

Cyrus tied the horses' lead ropes to an eroded pinnacle of rock that stood as tall as Barnabas, then he turned and said, "What now?"

"We have to find a way down into the gorge."

Barnabas started untying the book bags from the horse, and Cyrus said, "Brother, I suspect that any trails out here are going to be narrow and covered with slippery sand and gravel. Perhaps it is wiser to leave the books tied to the horse."

Barnabas leaned heavily against the bag. "I am tired. Perhaps...just this once..."

Barnabas hesitantly turned away from the books and picked his way along the edge of the precipice. After several moments, he said, "There. Is that a trail cut into the side of the gorge?"

Kalay said, "Looks like several trails to me. They seem to crisscross the cliff face. Let's find out if they're passable."

She strode ahead, followed the trail over the rim, and disappeared into the gorge. In less than ten heartbeats the sound of cascading rocks erupted.

"Kalay!" Cyrus called, and hurried over the edge.

Barnabas and Zarathan rushed after Cyrus. When they'd scrambled down the first treacherous gravel-slick incline, the trail leveled out and they saw Kalay and

Cyrus ten paces ahead. Kalay was pointing to something on the wall of the gorge.

Barnabas turned to the stone wall beside him. "Oh," he said softly. "Look, Zarathan."

Zarathan walked forward and his mouth dropped open. The entire cliff face was one tomb after another. Some were so old their entries were barely visible. It was as though over time the blocking stones had melded with the limestone cliff, becoming one. Other tombs appeared to be brand new.

"That's why this trail is here," Barnabas said. "The bottom of the gorge must have been used up first, and people had to start carving their family tombs higher and higher on the cliff."

"How old are these?" Zarathan asked in awe.

"Such tombs only date to the first century, or perhaps a few decades earlier."

"You mean, to around the time of our Lord?"

"Yes." Barnabas smoothed his hand over an elaborate carving that adorned the facade of a small tomb. "This is the Ben Hinnom family tomb."

"Hinnom? Like the valley?"

"I suspect it's the very same, or at least a relative."

Zarathan edged forward to look at the inscription. The moonlight was strong enough that he could see the letters perfectly.

Kalay and Cyrus had started walking down the trail again, and Barnabas said, "Let's not fall behind, brother."

The footing was so uneven that Zarathan often had to grab for one of Barnabas's flailing arms after he'd tripped.

"Forgive me, brother," Barnabas said on the fourth stumble. "My eyes are particularly bad at night."

"Just don't fall. It's a long way down."

Barnabas peered over the edge, nodded, and braced a hand against the cliff to steady himself as he slowly continued down the trail.

It took another half hour to reach the bottom of the gorge. In that time, they must have passed hundreds of tombs. The smallest were barely the length of Zarathan's forearm and he suspected they had been carved for children.

They walked up beside Cyrus and Kalay, and Barnabas said, "Surely there's no one after us at this time of night. Why don't we split up and see what we find down here."

"No," Cyrus ordered sharply. He had his fingers around the hilt of his sword, as though ready at any instant to draw it. "We stay together. Pick a direction and we'll all follow you."

Barnabas flapped his arms helplessly. "Very well, south."

"Zarathan?" Cyrus said. "I'll lead. You bring up the rear."

"Oh, for the sake of the Goddess Mother, let me do it!" Kalay said. "I'm much better with a knife than the bo—than Zarathan."

It intrigued Zarathan that she'd stopped short of calling him a boy. *I should have saved her life sooner.*

Cyrus paused, considering, then pulled a fine silver-handled knife from his belt and held it out to Zarathan, saying, "He'll be all right. Take this, brother."

Zarathan backpedaled. "Didn't that belong to one of the dead sicarii?"

Cyrus stretched his hand out farther. "It doesn't matter who it belonged to, you may need it."

Zarathan plucked it from Cyrus's palm with two fingers and gingerly tucked it into his belt. It looked very strange resting right beside his prayer rope.

Cyrus gave him a soldierly nod and turned around to head south. Barnabas followed behind him. As Kalay passed Zarathan, she gave him an incredulous look, grabbed a handful of her skirt, and held it up as she followed Barnabas down the winding path that led deeper into the gorge.

Seven hours later, when the full moon had traveled all the way across the sky and perched just above the western horizon, Kalay finally grew tired of listening to Zarathan's excessive yawning. He'd been alternately yawning, stumbling, and grumbling since midnight.

She swung around, glared at him, and jerked the knife from his belt. "Walk in front of me," she commanded. "I'm bringing up the rear now."

"That's my knife. Give it back!"

"You're barely awake. You couldn't guard your own backside. Now, go on, walk in front of me."

Cyrus turned at the commotion, saw Kalay with the knife, and looked genuinely relieved. He called, "Brother, could you take Barnabas's arm? I think he's as tired as you are. I don't want him to fall and hurt himself."

Zarathan tramped forward, roughly gripped Barnabas's arm, and said, "Come along. We'll hold each other up."

"Thank you, brother. I admit I can barely seem to put one foot in front of the other. I—"

Barnabas stopped suddenly, looked up, then lunged

for the cliff so fast he almost jerked Zarathan off his feet.

"Dear Lord," Zarathan gasped. "Why did you do that?"

Barnabas was panting, his gaze roving the tomb facade. "Cyrus! Please come...come and tell me what you see? My eyes...I'm n-not certain I—"

"I'm right here," Cyrus said as he strode to Barnabas's side and intently stared at the facade.

Barnabas turned to search Cyrus's face. "Is it? Is—is it what I think it is?"

Cyrus used his finger to trace out the symbol for all to see. "It's an inverted *V* tented over a circle."

Barnabas's knees started shaking. He staggered forward and propped his hands against the cliff to keep standing. Zarathan and Kalay both rushed up to make certain he was all right.

"Brother?" Zarathan examined his face. "Can I help you?"

"You're exhausted. Why don't you sit for a time," Kalay suggested, taking his arm to help steady him.

Barnabas did not even look at them. His eyes were riveted to the tomb. "It's the symbol of the *tekton*. The symbol that's on the map, marking the place where the Square of the Column stands."

A gust of wind swept the gorge and tousled Cyrus's curly black hair around his face. "Does it mean something?"

Barnabas straightened, pulled away from Zarathan and Kalay, and edged closer to the symbol. "It may mean...everything."

He gently caressed the lines of the symbol, as though trying to memorize every detail.

Cyrus watched him for a time, before asking, "What do you want me to do?"

"Open it. Hurry, before it gets light and someone can stop us."

Cyrus waved to Zarathan. "Brother, we'll both need to put our shoulders against the blocking stone and push."

Barnabas dropped to his knees to the left of the blocking stone and clasped his hands in prayer, murmuring while Zarathan and Cyrus pushed.

Kalay stood back.

It didn't take long. The blocking stone grated and scraped, and a musty rush of air escaped from the tomb. It sounded like the last breath of a dying man, and smelled similar.

Cyrus said, "It's open, brother. The moonlight is filling it up."

Barnabas struggled to his feet and hobbled forward to look inside. "We're lucky we didn't find it earlier. The moon would have been in a different position, and we'd never have seen the symbol of the *tekton*, let alone have light streaming into the tomb." Without another word, he ducked through the entry and disappeared inside.

Cyrus's gaze sought out Kalay. "I'll stand guard by the entrance. You go with my brothers. If there are inscriptions, they may need you to help translate the Hebrew."

Zarathan backed away. "Brother, I'd rather stay out here with you. I don't—"

"Zarathan," Cyrus said in a stern voice. "Barnabas is frail and tired. He doesn't see well in the dark. If he stumbles and falls, I doubt Kalay has the strength to get him on his feet again. He needs you in there."

Zarathan gulped a swallow, seemed to be mustering his courage, then resolutely walked forward and ducked into the tomb.

A loud gasp sounded, followed by Zarathan's frightened voice: "There are skulls on the floor in here!"

"Well, don't break them!" Kalay called back.

She remained outside for a time, staring at Cyrus. Even in the moonlight, his emerald eyes glittered when he looked at her. Softly, she said, "We are probably not alone out here. You know that, don't you? They almost certainly followed us."

A slow, radiant smile turned his lips—the smile of a man who's already given himself up for dead. "Yes. I know."

Annoyed, she snapped, "Get that martyr's smile off your face. You're not going to die unless you start taking reckless chances."

His smile widened. "This entire trip is one big reckless chance."

"Yes, well, there is that, but I order you to call out immediately if you hear or see anything suspicious."

He nodded obediently. "I will. Kalay, can you..." He hesitated. "If you find anything important, will you come out and tell me?"

He obviously longed to be one of the chosen to enter the tomb, to see what it contained for himself. But he trusted no one else to protect them from the evils that might lurk in the night.

"Don't worry," she said. "If we find something inscribed with the words THE PEARL, I'll bring it right out to you."

He gave her a mildly irritated look. "Thank you."
She grinned and ducked into the tomb.

22

Loukas, on his belly, slid back from the precipice, and whispered to Elicius, "Pappas Meridias is probably staying in the new monastery being built north of the city. Find him. Tell him we believe they have found it, and he should bring at least ten men to surround the tomb. Twenty would be better."

"Yes," Elicius said, and tossed windblown gray hair out of his eyes. "Just the sight of twenty armed men will take the fight out of Atinius."

When Elicius kept lying there, smiling, Loukas said, "Now. Go now. And pick up those two men we saw guarding that open tomb. We'll need every man."

Elicius's mouth pursed, but he got to his feet and silently trotted away into the darkness.

Alexander glared at Loukas, as though he didn't much like the way he treated his friend Elicius.

Loukas slid forward to the edge of the precipice again and watched Atinius standing guard in front of the tomb. The gorge was deep and narrow, the rocky footing treacherous. The fool. With one well-placed arrow, an archer could kill him, then block the tomb and trap his friends inside. Even if they escaped, no one could run far or fast in these eroded limestone outcrops. They could be easily hunted down and killed. What was Atinius thinking?

But he's surprised me before.

Loukas turned to Alexander. "Stay here. Signal the soldiers when they come. I'm going to take my horse, go around, and block the mouth of the gorge below, so they can't possibly escape."

23

NISAN THE 18TH, THE YEAR 3771

I see her the instant we ride to the edge of the gorge. In the moonlight, the pale limestone cliffs have a liquid silver shine. She sits far below, in front of the tekton's tomb. Her himation is pulled over her head, and she is rocking back and forth. The breeze carries the faint sound of her mourning cries.

"Leave the horses to graze," I tell Titus. "Come with me."

We dismount and carefully make our way down the narrow trail that leads to the bottom of the gorge. Along the way, I touch the tombs of people I have known and loved. People I miss.

We reach the trail in the gorge bottom where the footing is better, though still precarious, and I quicken my pace. Ahead, the symbol of the tekton, carved only a few days ago by Yeshua, reflects the moonlight, glowing as though lit from behind.

She looks up when we stop before her. Long black

hair fringes the edges of her himation, and frames her swollen face. In her eyes, I do not see surprise, but utter despair.

I crouch beside her. "Maryam," I softly say. " You did well. I spoke to Lazaros. He told me—"

"You don't know the whole truth, Yosef," she says in a grief-stricken voice. "Forgive me, I—I deceived you."

I reach out to touch her hand. "I know part of it. We were ambushed by Roman soldiers at dusk tonight, just outside of Emmaus. They cut the burial shroud open. We saw the man we carried."

Her wet eyes widen, and tears trace lines down her cheeks. "You saw him?"

"Dysmas, yes."

"Did you"—she wipes her cheeks with the corner of her himation—"did you take care of him? "

It was so like her to worry as much about the soul of a crucified murderer as she would the soul of a saint.

I gently say, "If you love them that love you, what reward have you?"

Her mouth quivers.

I smile. "We did the best we could for him. We buried him in a beautiful pomegranate orchard. I prayed for his soul. The rest is in God's hands."

In a tender, almost lover-like gesture, she reaches out and clasps my hand. "He would be grateful, Yosef, as I am."

I know she means Yeshua, not Dysmas, and her words bring tears to my eyes.

"Yosef, please try to understand. You helped us so much, helped...him...so much. I couldn't take the chance that if they caught you, you would bear the brunt of the

praefectus's wrath. So, I..." She lowers her gaze, as though ashamed of her deception.

"You alone took the risk." I expel a breath and close my eyes for several long moments, letting her bravery sink into my heart before I say, *"Maryam, truly, you are the greatest of his disciples. You made his teachings a part of you. He would be very proud."*

A sob lodges in her throat. She closes her eyes, trying not to make a sound.

I give her some time. Then I ask, *"What will you do now? You mustn't stay in Yerushalaim. It's too dangerous."*

She swallows hard. *"I'm going to the Galil. A friend told me that's where Kepha has gone. I must face him. Yosef, I'm sure he's the one who—"*

"As I am." Anger stirs the ashes of my grief. *"Do you want me to go with you?"*

She shakes her head. *"No, I must do it alone. And you must leave, Yosef. Tonight. The Council is looking for you, and the praefectus—"*

"Yes, Lazaros told me. If I stay, I fully expect to be arrested."[1]

A cloud passes across the face of the moon, and the gorge is shrouded in utter darkness.

"Master," Titus says. His curly brown hair looks gray tonight, making him seem older. *"I know you could not tell me the whole truth when this began, but now—"*

"Yes." I exhale the word. *"Now it's time you understood. You deserve the truth more than anyone."*

He waits, watching me. Occasionally, he glances at Maryam.

"Gamliel...he said it would take something monumental to stop the revolt, something so stunning that the

shocked crowds would forget their anger and lay down their arms to embrace each other."

Titus appears to be thinking about that, his mind working through the maze of information. A cool breeze blows up the Kidron valley and flattens his robe against his chest. "You mean it had to be the fulfillment of prophecy?"

I glance at Maryam. When she says nothing, I add, "We knew that many people would think he'd escaped, and many more that his body had been stolen, but the faithful, those looking for the coming of the messiah..."

In an awed whisper, Titus says, "They would believe."

Maryam breathes, "With all their hearts."

I wait for him to ask more. When he does not, I rise to my feet and look at the tomb.

Maryam begins rocking again, back and forth.

"Is he in there?" I ask. "Is that where you put him?"

Why else would she be here?

She closes her eyes, and her shoulders heave. When she gains control, she says, "It is his family tomb. He carved the facade just days before his arrest." Her hoarse voice trails away.

I lift my gaze to the symbol of the tekton. His grandfather, and his great-grandfather, and more fathers back into the dark mists of time, were excellent stoneworkers. He would rejoice to be with them. It is a fitting place.

I just stare at it for a time, remembering the sound of his deep voice.

Finally, I bow my head and pray, "Happy are they who dwell in the Lord's House, they shall be ever praising thee! Happy the people that is so circumstanced, happy the people whose God is the Eternal. I extol thee, my God, my King, and bless thy name evermore."

Maryam, surprised, lifts her head. Together, she and Titus reply in unison, "Let the name of the Eternal be praised, and exalted in his name alone. Amayne."

A trembling smile touches Maryam's lips. She rises unsteadily to her feet and turns, with me, to face the tomb as I begin the Yiskor, the burial service.

The setting is wrong. I cannot do everything I need to. But what little I can offer is better than nothing.

I take a deep breath, and sing in a soft voice, "May God remember the soul of our honored teacher, Yeshua ben Pantera...."

24

The moonlight shining into the tomb was dazzling. It was as though it had been carved in anticipation of this exact moment.

As Kalay's eyes adjusted, she studied the squarish shape of the main burial chamber. There were three skulls on the floor; each rested before a loculus, or in Hebrew, *kokh*, a tunnel carved into the wall where ossuaries were placed on rock shelves. There were six *kokhim*. Even from here, near the entry, she could count several bone boxes in the recesses.

In a strained voice, Barnabas said, "Kalay, please, let me read this to you."

She walked through the silver wash of light to where Barnabas and Zarathan crouched before a rectangular box carved from limestone. Back in the tunnel, she counted two more ossuaries.

Barnabas said, "I can't see very well, but I believe this one says, *Yuda bar Yeshua.*"

Kalay translated, "Iuda son of Iesous."

Zarathan stared at her, aghast. "Our Lord had a son?"

Barnabas shook his head. "It may mean nothing, Zarathan. Let's keep looking."

He crawled deeper into the tunnel and read aloud: "Here's one marked *Yose* and another, *Maria*."

"Our Lord's parents!" Zarathan looked like he might faint.

Kalay shook her head. "Those are two of the most common names in the history of the Ioudaiosoi, you idiot. They don't mean anything."

"There's also a *Mariamne* back here," Barnabas called. "The inscription is in Greek, which is a little curious."

Kalay looked straight at Zarathan and hissed, "That's probably one of your Lord's sisters that you don't believe in."

"I didn't say I didn't believe!"

Barnabas crawled out and moved to another tunnel. He reached into it, turned one of the ossuaries, and leaned so close to the inscription his nose almost touched the box. He haltingly read, *"Yakob...bar Yosef... achui de...Yeshua."*

Kalay grinned at Zarathan. "Iakobos, son of Ioses, brother of Iesous."

When Zarathan fell back against the wall with his mouth agape, Kalay said, "Obviously, your Lord's brother—er, cousin."

In a strangled voice, Zarathan said, "I don't believe it!"

Barnabas continued moving around the tomb. "These have no inscriptions," he said after searching three ossuaries.

As he moved to the fourth tunnel, he sucked in a deep breath and placed a hand against the wall, as though to gather his failing strength. They'd been up all night, eaten nothing in two days, and been traveling hard. She was amazed he'd made it this far.

"Brother," Kalay called. "Please sit down and rest for just a few moments. Otherwise, I'm afraid you're going to fall down."

"No, no, I...I can't. There's no way of knowing how much time we have."

Zarathan righted himself, blinked as though waking, and marched across the room to take Barnabas's arm. "Forgive me, brother, I should have been helping you all along."

"Thank you, Zarathan," Barnabas said and leaned on his brother as he moved to the next tunnel.

The ossuary in front sat in a particularly bright patch of moonlight. It seemed impossible that such a thing could be an accident. Had the person who'd placed it here done it at night? With moonlight streaming through the entry just like this?

Barnabas got down on his knees to examine it. "There's an inscription," he said, "but it's difficult to make out." He sounded out the letters for a time, then in a shaking voice read, *"Yeshua...bar...Yosef."*[1]

Zarathan let out a small cry and spun around to stare at Kalay. "I *told* you Ioses was his father! I knew it!"

"Zarathan, do you know how common these names are?"

"B-but all of them!" Zarathan stammered. "All of them in one place? This must have been Iesous's family tomb!"

Kalay folded her arms. "That means you'll have to admit that your Lord had a son. Hmm. Then maybe that Mariamne was the one known as the Magdalen. Yuda's mother?"

It might have been the moonlight, but she swore that Zarathan's young face lost all color. "No," he whispered. "I don't believe it. I *won't* believe it!"

Barnabas said, "There's another inscribed tomb back here."

Kalay asked, "What does it say?"

He squinted hard. "It might be...*Matya.*"

"Oh, there's a ringer for you, Zarathan." Kalay's brows lifted. "In Greek that's *Maththaios.* Why would there be a Maththaios in Iesous's family tomb?"

Zarathan wet his lips, and breathed before he said, "Maybe he was the son of Yuda or some other family member who lived later?"

"Now you're thinking," she said, and shoved a lock of long red hair from her eyes. "Maybe all of these are from a later time. Maybe decades, or centuries later. Even yesterday—"

"No," Barnabas corrected as he grabbed Zarathan's wrist to steady himself. "Decades, perhaps, but we know that this burial tradition dates only to the time just before and just after our Lord was alive."

"See, I told you," Zarathan stubbornly insisted. "It's Iesous's family tomb!"

Kalay gestured to Barnabas's hand where it clutched Zarathan's wrist. "Best let go, Barnabas. Your grip's jeopardizing the blood flow to his brain."

Barnabas turned and his face glowed with deep reverence. Softly, he said, "The likelihood that the map would lead us here, and that all these names would occur in one tomb and not be associated with our Lord...well, it's virtually impossible."

"Brother Barnabas," she said as though reprimanding a child. "Do you know how many members of my own family have these names?"

He blinked. "No."

"I have a cousin named *Yeshua ben Yosef.* My three aunts are named *Mari, Maryam,* and *Miryam.* My grandfather was *Yakob*"—she took a breath to continue her litany—"I have three second cousins named *Yuda.* And the number of men named *Matya*—well, too many to count."

Zarathan's jaw had locked, and his eyes narrowed like a wild pig's just before it charges. "There are ten ossuaries in this tomb, and five have inscriptions that bear the names of our Lord's family. This is no accident. You're just trying to demean—"

"I surrender," she said and threw up her hands. "You've found the Pearl. Let's go home to Egypt."

Kalay stalked across the chamber and ducked outside into the night.

Cyrus, who stood three paces away, spun breathlessly, waiting for her to tell him what they'd discovered.

"Yes?"

The wind still gusted wildly, flinging sand and gravel in every direction.

She strode to him and said, "Go see for yourself. There's an ossuary in there that bears the inscription *Yeshua bar Yosef.*"

His anxious expression slackened, and his eyes went wide and wet with faith. For several moments, he was unable to speak. Finally, he whispered, "Truly?"

"Yes, absolutely. Go and see it. I'll stand guard for the few moments it will take you."

Cyrus hesitated. He clearly wanted to go inside, but was uncertain he could leave his post.

"Go on," she ordered and made a shooing motion with her hands.

Cyrus grimaced, then broke. He rushed past her and ducked into the tomb.

Voices rose and carried on the wind, filled with awe and conviction. Several instants later, someone started crying, barely audible. She thought it was Barnabas. Then Zarathan let out a deep-throated sob, and burst into tears.

Kalay drew the knife from her belt and walked a few paces down the gorge. There, in the shadows, she leaned heavily against the cliff. The moon had almost sunk below the western horizon and the first rays of dawn filtered through the sky like pale blue smoke.

She took a deep breath and let it out slowly. What fools men were. A few names scribbled on rocks and they went to pieces.

Though, she had to admit, they were intriguing names.

She tried to imagine what the monks would do if they all agreed the ossuary was the Pearl. Would they pack it up and haul it home to place on the altar of a new monastery? Perhaps they would open it, and each start carrying around finger bones; "relics," they were called. That was such a ghastly thought. She took a few more steps down the gorge.

Just ahead of her a cascade of pebbles bounced down the cliff, and Kalay craned her neck to scan the stone wall high above. The ferocious wind had probably scooped it from a ledge ... but an old and familiar chill crept about her bones. It was like hearing a footfall in a room that's supposed to be empty.

She turned to study the black pool of moon shadow across the gorge where a small sandstorm spun. There was nothing there. Nothing.

Then...a whisper of leather and metal, a sudden glint of silver.

Instinctively, she spun with her knife held low and slashed straight into the downward arc of a sword. The impact knocked her blade to the ground and left her hand stinging. Madly, she grabbed for the bronze dagger that remained in her belt and fell into a crouch.

Loukas laughed and circled her. "You must have known I'd find you," he said. His reddish-blond hair looked pewter in the moonlight, and his broad nose shone, as though covered with sweat. "I hope you've been preparing yourself for this moment. I have."

Kalay lunged at him with the dagger.

Loukas countered with the flat of his sword, bashing her hand, sending the dagger spinning off into the darkness. A cruel smile turned his lips.

She ran headlong down the narrow gorge, her heart pounding to the sound of his boots crashing on the dry gravel behind her. She fought to think, to—

Just as she started to scream, a hand clamped hard over her mouth, jerked her backward, and a muscular arm tightened against her throat.

In her ear, he whispered, "Be quiet, *beauty*. Don't struggle. Or I'll see that your friends die very slowly."

As he gagged her, bound her hands behind her, and tied her ankles, she shot a frantic glance up the gorge, expecting to see Cyrus stepping outside.

"That's a good girl," Loukas hissed as he pulled the ropes so tight they cut into her flesh like rusty knives.

Then he forced her to walk down the gorge to where a horse stood hidden in the shadows. By the time he finally muscled her onto the horse's back and took off at a fast trot, she could barely breathe.

As they galloped away, she heard horses. Many horses. Coming fast.

She had to twist around to look.

High above, flooding out of the Dung Gate, were at least two decuria, and perhaps another ten men dressed in religious robes.

Loukas quickly reined his horse down into a small shadowed drainage that emptied off to one side.

Kalay wrenched her body and tried to scream, to get someone's attention, maybe she could distract the soldiers long enough for—

Loukas slammed a fist into the back of her neck, almost knocking her unconscious. "Don't try it!" he hissed. "Your friends are doomed. You had better start thinking of yourself, and what you can do to make me forget that shed in Leontopolis."

Kalay closed her eyes.

25

Zarathan slumped down on the rock shelf in front of one of the uninscribed ossuaries and watched Cyrus and Barnabas where they stood talking and gently touching the box marked YESHUA BAR YOSEF.[1] The last half hour with the three of them together had been like a revelation. That same divine bliss that came over him when he'd prayed all night now filled his heart, but even more powerfully; it was an ineffable radiance, a peace such as he had never known.

He looked around. They'd gone over each ossuary again with Cyrus, and he'd added his own knowledge of the people whose names were written on them. Zarathan felt for the first time as though he truly knew these long-dead saints.

They had decided that the tomb simply marked YOSE may have been their Lord's brother, rather than his adopted father, which conveniently settled a dispute, and that Yuda bar Yeshua was probably a relative from a decade or two later. His ossuary did seem different. It was smaller and more crudely carved. Maria and Mariamne were likely his mother and sister. Matya was still a mystery, one that, even now, Cyrus and Barnabas quietly debated.

"It's possible that he might have been the disciple known as Levi, but if this is our Lord's family tomb, it seems unlikely the former tax collector would be here and none of the other disciples would be."

Cyrus was smoothing his hand over the Yeshua bar Yosef ossuary as though touching a lover. "I agree. Again, it could be a family member from the same time as Yuda. Perhaps even Yuda's brother."

Cyrus's deep voice had a strange resonance, a kindness that left Zarathan trembling.

The wind outside increased to a roar and a fierce gust swept into the tomb and blew around the ossuaries like a ghost, kicking up dust.

As though something had just occurred to Cyrus, he jerked his hand away from the ossuary, whirled toward the entry, and his eyes went huge. "Kalay! I forgot! Brothers, stay here. I'll be right back!"

He ran for the entry and ducked outside into the howling gale.

Barnabas stared after him, then he glanced at Zarathan. "I'm sure she's well."

But in a quarter hour, when neither Cyrus nor Kalay had returned, Barnabas began to grow anxious. He walked to the entry and peered outside. The moonlight had given way to a cerulean hue, heralding the coming of dawn.

Barnabas turned back to Zarathan, took two steps, and opened his mouth to—

A tall body blocked the entry, and Zarathan could see several other men behind, filling the gorge.

"Brother!" Zarathan cried as he leaped off the stone shelf and stared wide-eyed over Barnabas's shoulder.

Barnabas swung around.

Four Roman soldiers ducked into the tomb and took up positions around the chamber, their swords drawn. They wore bronze helmets and held the shields of the legion. The clinking of all the metal sounded loud in the quiet tomb.

Two other men, both dressed in the black robes of bishops, entered after them.

The tall, younger bishop had short blond hair and a clean-shaven face. The older man was short with wispy brown hair and heavy jowls. He looked to be about Barnabas's age.

Barnabas said, "Who are you?"

The blond bishop extended a hand to the other man. "This is Pappas Macarios of Jerusalem. I believe you remember me, don't you, Brother Barnabas?"

Barnabas stared daggers at Meridias.

Macarios glanced between the two men, then bowed slightly to Barnabas. "Brothers, greetings in the name of our Lord. Do you—"

Meridias interrupted, "What are you two doing here?"

Barnabas folded his hands in front of him and Zarathan wondered if he was thinking about the dead monks in Egypt, many of whom Barnabas had known and loved for twenty years. In a matter-of-fact voice, Barnabas said, "You know very well what we're doing here, Meridias. We're searching for the Pearl."

Macarios frowned as though confused, but he

looked excessively nervous. Despite the wind and cold, his forehead glistened with sweat. "I don't know what that is." Macarios turned to Meridias for an explanation.

Meridias didn't look at him. He kept his narrowed gaze on Barnabas. "And did you find it?"

"Of course not. It's a legend. A fantasy created by some cruel prankster three centuries ago." Barnabas pulled the papyrus from his pocket and threw it on the floor. "There's the map, if you want it."

Meridias gestured for Macarios to pick it up. The elderly little bishop stooped, grasped it, and looked at it briefly before he handed it to Meridias.

Zarathan couldn't speak. He stared at the map in Meridias's hand in horror. The man who'd destroyed their monastery, killed their brothers, was now holding the sacred artifact. It was almost too much to bear.

Meridias glanced at Zarathan. "You. Boy. Why are you crying?"

Zarathan planted his feet, swallowed hard, his mind racing. "I—I'm sad because we didn't find the Pearl."

Again Macarios said, "What is the Pearl?"

Impatiently, Meridias said, "No one knows, it's—"

"It was supposed to be the tomb of our Lord, Iesous Christos," Barnabas said to Macarios. "Just foolishness."

A stunned look of reverence came over Macarios's face. "And—and the map led you here?"

"If we followed it correctly, yes. Though I'm still not certain we did. However, the ossuaries in this tomb do make one wonder."

"What do you mean?" Macarios took a step forward.

Barnabas gripped Macarios's arm and led him around the chamber, reading the inscriptions aloud. Macarios's expression grew more awed with each name.

Zarathan knew how he felt, but Pappas Meridias seemed totally unaffected...until they came to the tomb inscribed YESHUA BAR YOSEF.

Meridias shouted, *"What?* Is that correct? Macarios, you read it. Is that what it really says?"

Macarios leaned down to study the inscription. After several agonizing moments, he straightened. "Yes, that's what it says."

Meridias spun around to the soldiers and ordered, "Crush every one of these ossuaries and scatter the shards in the desert. Then come back to destroy this tomb! I want it—"

"Why?" Macarios asked in a calm, inquiring voice.

"Don't ask me idiotic questions. I give the orders here. Decurion, arrest these men!"

The decurion marched toward Barnabas and grabbed hold of his sleeve.

"Wait, Rufus," Macarios said almost casually to the decurion, and it occurred to Zarathan that the soldier was, of course, stationed in Jerusalem, and therefore accustomed to obeying Macarios. "There's no reason to arrest these men. These ossuaries are nothing special."

The decurion released Barnabas.

Meridias looked to be on the verge of exploding. He yelled, "What are you *talking* about? If the bones of Iesous Christos are in that box, don't you see what it will do to our Church!"

"Pappas." Macarios sighed. "Your reaction is understandable, but it is misguided. I have two ossuaries in my office at the monastery inscribed in exactly the same way, *Yeshua bar Yosef.* When we return, I will be happy to show them to you."

Meridias seemed totally taken aback. He glanced around the chamber, as though he feared he were the butt of some terrible joke. "Two?"

Macarios gave him an indulgent smile. "We have recovered over two thousand ossuaries from the hills around Jerusalem. From the written information as well as the ossuaries we've gleaned, we have determined that perhaps one thousand men in Jerusalem at the time of our Lord were named Yeshua and had fathers named Yosef."

Angrily, Meridias said, "And what about Yakob son of Yosef, brother of Yeshua? Surely there can't have been many men who carried such a name."

"No, that's true. But I estimate perhaps twenty or twenty-five.[2] These names are extremely common. Why, consider the names Maria and Mariamne in the back loculus. Both are variations of the Hebrew name Miriam, which was the most common female name of the first century. And the names Yakob, Yosef, Yudah, Yeshua, and Matya were so common that we believe perhaps forty percent of all men at the time carried those names."

Zarathan's heart began to sink. Macarios almost had him convinced, and Meridias seemed totally confused. He'd started pacing like a madman.

"Pappas Meridias, think of the holy Roman Empire. How many men are named Gaius, Julius, Marcus, Lucius, or Septus? Thousands in the city of Rome alone."

Meridias gaped at Macarios in disbelief.

The short priest put a hand on the decurion's shoulder and gently said, "Rufus, please take your men and return to the monastery. You're not needed here."

"Yes, Pappas."

As the decurion motioned to his men and they began to file out of the tomb, Meridias cried, "Wait! I haven't dismissed you!"

The soldiers paid him no attention. One by one they ducked outside, and the decurion's voice rose above the wind: "Climb the trail. We're returning to the city!"

Only one man remained guarding the entry. A gray-haired old man that Zarathan recognized as one of the men who'd attacked them at Libni's caves.

A dangerous brew of terror and rage boiled in his veins. If only he could get his hands around the man's throat! Memories flashed of the fight on the beach, of all the fear and pain they'd endured...so powerful was the need to hurt in return, that it took all of his control to remain in place.

Barnabas said, "Pappas Macarios, I'm sure we broke some law when we entered this tomb. Whatever penalties you judge appropriate, we will of course submit to without argument."

Macarios thoughtfully fingered his beard. "It is illegal to damage graves, or steal grave goods, but"—he looked around—"I see no evidence that you did either. You opened the tomb, yes, and that showed poor judgment on your part, but you did no harm."

"You're very gracious, Pappas." Barnabas kneeled before him and kissed the man's hand. "Forgive us for causing such an unintended uproar."

Meridias stared at them with narrowed eyes. He

spun on his heel, stalked out of the tomb, and shouted, "Elicius, we're leaving!"

When the sound of their footsteps died away, Barnabas rose to his feet, faced Macarios, and a slow smile came to his face. Barnabas whispered, "You received the message I sent from Gaza?"

Macarios chuckled softly. "I did."

Macarios spread his arms, and the two men embraced like lifelong friends.

Zarathan gaped. He stumbled in his haste to reach the entry and look outside. When he was certain no one stood close enough to see them, he hissed, "Do you know each other?"

Barnabas said, "Macarios and I were both library assistants in Caesarea—"

"Along with several others," Macarios clarified.

Tears welled in Barnabas's eyes when he looked at his old friend. "When I heard they were hunting us down, I was desperately afraid you would be one of the first they'd find. You are so visible."

"Yes, but I've made a point of supporting Pappas Silvester's every whim. I wasn't worried about me, but you? I was sure they'd kill you. You are known far and wide as Barnabas the Heretic." Macarios chuckled again, then his voice lowered. "Do you know anything of the fates of Libni and Symeon? Are they well?"

Barnabas expelled a breath. "I know nothing of Symeon, but when we left Libni, he was gravely wounded. He—"

"Meridias's work?"

"Almost certainly."

Macarios clamped his jaw and looked away as though considering what to do. After a time, his gaze darted around the tomb, and he whispered, "When I received your warning and the message about what had happened at your monastery, I began my own search. Of course, I've been at it for years, as you have, but I believe I have uncovered something important."

Barnabas eyed him for several heartbeats, then stepped back. "More important than this tomb?"

"Maybe. I'm not sure yet. I had two of my most loyal monks excavating when Meridias arrived. They had to abandon their work and make it appear as though grave robbers had broken into the tomb, but—"

Barnabas sucked in a sudden breath. "The short leg? On the map? You found what lies at the end of the short leg!"

Macarios held up a hand. "Don't get your hopes up. I *may* have. But we've barely begun to explore the Shroud Tomb. Meridias himself entered it, but the man is too dim-witted to understand what he was seeing." His expression tightened. "He's ordered it resealed. I'll have to stall."

Zarathan ducked out to inspect the gorge outside one more time, then turned. "Brothers, we must find Cyrus and Kalay. They are nowhere to be seen."

Barnabas said, "Macarios, I may need your help again. We—"

"You have it without asking. You know that. Why don't we head for the Shroud Tomb and you can tell me about your friends on the way."

Barnabas nodded, but his eyes drifted around the tomb again, landing on each of the ossuaries, and a soft light shone in his eyes. "Are you sure this isn't it? It—it feels right. Holy."

"It is holy. But as to whether this is our Lord's family tomb...I cannot say for certain."

"No," Barnabas whispered. "No, I suppose not."

As they walked toward the entry, Macarios affectionately put his arm around Barnabas's shoulders. "Still, it might be."

26

Kalay didn't know how long they'd been riding. It seemed only moments, but when Loukas dragged her off the horse, her legs felt like boiled straw. She could barely stand. He'd struck her harder than she'd thought.

They were on the slope, just at the brow overlooking the gorge. She recognized another of the numerous tombs, this one freshly opened, with loose dirt piled beside the dark opening. She ground her teeth in an effort to chew through the cloth he'd tied tightly around her head to gag her.

Loukas picked her up and carried her to the tomb. He shoved her through the small entrance, heedless of banging her against the stone. She almost tumbled down the stairs, squirming to keep from knocking her head.

Loukas stepped over her and reached down to drag her across the rough limestone floor. Then he shoved her onto a rock shelf near two ossuaries. He was smiling as he climbed the steps and went outside again.

While he was gone, and she heard him rummaging through the pack on the horse, she rolled to the floor, sat down, and managed to slip her hands beneath her hips, then her feet. When they were in front of her, she frantically started trying to untie the knots.

Loukas returned with a burning oil lamp, saw her, and made a disappointed clucking sound. As he calmly set the oil lamp on an ossuary, he said, "I can see you're going to be a problem." With lightning speed, he backhanded her.

Kalay tumbled across the floor.

When she opened her eyes, she caught sight of a shrouded skeleton lying on the shelf above her. *I'll probably be up there with you soon, friend. After what I did to him in Leontopolis, he's not going to keep me for long.*

Loukas carried the oil lamp into another chamber. When he returned, he kneeled in front of her and stroked her hair with a gloved hand. *"Soon."*

He roughly grabbed her by her bound feet and dragged her into the next chamber, where the oil lamp cast a faint amber glow over another dozen ossuaries.

As he glared down at her, Kalay didn't move. She just stared back, reading his hatred, breathing hard, trying not to think about the future.

The lamplight flickered, and she noticed small things. There was a strange, spicy scent that seemed to ooze from the walls, probably myrrh and aloes, maybe frankincense. And the ossuaries here were elaborately decorated, not like the plain, inscribed boxes in the *tekton's* tomb. These had domed lids with exquisite carvings around the rims and gorgeous interlinked rosettes cut into the sides. Many were painted. A master stoneworker had carved these. In the far corner, almost hidden by shattered ossuaries, was a sealed doorway, or the top of a doorway. It was as though there had originally been a third, lower level, and this chamber was built over the top of it, forever sealing the lower chamber, except for maybe one cubit of the old doorway.

Loukas tugged his robe over his head and stood naked before her. His healed scrotum looked lopsided with its missing testicle, but his rising penis left no illusions about his intentions. He had arms as big around as her waist. As he knelt and cut the ropes binding her ankles, she wildly kicked him in the head, rolled to her feet, and made a mad run for the door.

He tackled her, bringing her down hard. She screamed against her gag, kicked him, and as a last act of defiance slammed him in the face with her forehead. When he finally pinned her arms and legs with his heavy body, his face was bleeding, but his eyes ... his eyes were alight.

"Oh, I look forward to watching you suffer. You took half of me in Egypt. Before I'm done, there will be nothing left of you but a bloody shell."

Kalay locked her jaw as he viciously jerked her dress up past her waist. A hard slap dazed her enough that he could force her legs apart. He was watching her intently as he drove himself inside her. His thrusts were wild and brutal, designed to hurt her, to make her cry out.

Her entire body screamed at the hurt and outrage, but she bit back the cries that rose in her throat.

Instead, Kalay sought an old refuge, one she hadn't used in many years. It was a dark, quiet place inside her. As a child, she'd built it, brick by brick, creating a sanctuary from men, one she could return to in the worst of times, when she felt utterly hopeless.

She closed her eyes and with all of her strength sought to abandon her body. She sent her soul traveling down into that brilliant darkness, far away from here, from his stinking body, from—

A voice filtered through the chamber. Soft, calling out. A man's voice. She couldn't understand the words, but she knew it was a question.

She opened her eyes. Loukas didn't seem to hear it. He'd started to pant and move faster, and his eyes had that glazed look she'd seen on the faces of so many men.

The voice came again, this time louder, more mournful, as though pleading for someone to hear him.

To her right, a tiny flash of light sparked near the floor.

She jerked her head sideways to try to find the place it had come from.

"Move," Loukas ordered. "Move or I'll tear your heart out."

She moved.

His frenzy built. He buried his face against her shoulder and began grunting and groaning, writhing on top of her.

Footsteps.

She heard footsteps.

... and that voice again, this time it was frantic, almost shouting. The words lay just beyond her ability to hear.

Pure terror fired her veins.

Another flash of light to her right. She didn't have time to look. Loukas stiffened and cried out, and a massive shadow crossed in front of the lamplight, hurling down.

Kalay screamed into her gag and barely jerked aside as Loukas's head smacked face-first into the floor, bounced off the stone, then was pounded down again.

"Get out of the way, Kalay!"

As the heavy ossuary lifted again, she glimpsed Cyrus's face, his eyes wild with rage. She shoved out from under Loukas and rolled away.

Blow after blow, Cyrus pounded Loukas's head until there was little more than pulp remaining. When the ossuary cracked on the final blow, and shards cartwheeled across the floor, Cyrus dropped the chunks he still held and stumbled backward.

For a long while, he stared at the body, waiting until the arms and legs stopped jerking. When he knew the man was dead, his gaze lifted to Kalay.

She made a muffled sound through her gag.

Without a word, Cyrus pulled his knife and went to her, sawing first through her gag, then the ropes tying her hands. When she was free, he said, "Forgive me," pulled her into his arms, and ferociously crushed her body against his. She felt him shaking, as though on the verge of tears.

She sank against him, her relief so great she couldn't seem to think. "I thought you were dead."

"I shouldn't have left you alone out there. I started looking at the ossuaries and I lost track of—"

"Cyrus?" She suddenly remembered the soldiers. "Where are Barnabas and Zarathan?"

He released her. "As soon as I realized you were missing, I ran to the top of the cliff and grabbed one of the horses, then I saw the soldiers riding down the slope and had to hide until they'd passed."

"You left your brothers to face the soldiers alone and came after me?"

His jaw clenched for a moment and she could see the turmoil, the admission he didn't want to make. "It was too late, Kalay. There were too many of them. I wouldn't have been of any use there."

"But how did you find me?"

He cocked his head as though the question were absurd. "I heard you calling me."

"Calling you?"

"Yes."

"What are you talking about?"

His brows pulled together. "You shouted my name. Over and over. I heard you from halfway across the Kidron valley."

"Cyrus, I...I was gagged."

His eyes darted to the gag on the floor. He'd cut and pulled it from her mouth only moments ago. He stared at the soggy cloth as though it were impossible. "Then, who called me here?"

Kalay's gaze went to the bricked-up doorway across the room. That's where the flashes of light had come from. She was sure of it.

Cyrus followed her gaze. "What is that? An old doorway?"

Shooting Loukas's corpse an angry glare, she struggled to her feet. "I swear I saw something.... Help me open it."

27

This is the stone which was not set by you builders, which has become the cornerstone.

— ACTS 4:11

By the time Macarios had led them to the Shroud Tomb, the wind had almost vanished, and the cloudless morning sky was shot through with pink lances of light that radiated outward from the golden halo on the rugged eastern horizon. The sweet scent of freshly sprouted wheat fields carried on the breeze.

As they rode over a rise, Barnabas saw the open tomb down in the Hinnom valley. He swiveled around on his horse and, in his mind, drew a line from the Dung Gate to the tomb.

"It's possible," he whispered, but feared to hope.

For the first time in many years, he felt alone. From the moment they'd left the *tektons* tomb, a black emptiness had begun filling him, until now he feared it would suffocate him. He had failed. The entire Occultum Lapidem had been a farce. There was no hidden stone. But many men—good, faithful men—had died to help him protect what was hidden at the end of the papyrus map. How would God ever forgive him? How would he ever forgive himself?

He kicked his horse into a trot, calling to the bishop who rode the horse in front of him, "Macarios, what is in this Shroud Tomb?"

Macarios slowed his horse so he could ride alongside Barnabas and Zarathan. "The ossuaries are extraordinary, much more elaborate than those in the *tektons* tomb. I only got to look at them briefly, but two of the boxes are inscribed with the names Mari and Salome."

"Possibly our Lord's sisters?"

"Possibly, but again, both names were common in the first century."

As they rode down the hill for the tomb, Barnabas asked, "Why do you call it the Shroud Tomb?"

"In the rear of the tomb, there's a body laid out on a shelf, still wrapped in the original burial linens. It's an amazing sight. Though sad."

"Why sad?" Zarathan asked from where he rode behind Barnabas.

"His family laid him out as was customary, but they never returned to finish the ritual burial, to clean his bones and place him in an ossuary. If you believe that the soul rests in the body until the resurrection, he's probably still waiting for his loved ones to come back and care for him."

Macarios rode to a stop in front of the tomb, studied the two horses that wandered through a garden of wind-sculpted boulders in the distance, and gave Barnabas a warning glance. "Do you recognize those animals?"

Barnabas felt as though a huge hand had reached out and squeezed his heart. In a whisper he said, "The horse with the big bags strapped over its withers belongs to Cyrus, the other monk with us."

"Just one of the beasts?"

"Yes, I don't know the second."

Barnabas and Zarathan dismounted and walked to stand beside Macarios near the entry. The tomb was deathly quiet.

Barnabas turned to Zarathan. "Brother, could you go and retrieve the horses? We may need them in a hurry."

"Yes, of course, brother." Zarathan started down the hill at a trot toward where the horses grazed among the standing stones.

"Let me go in first," Barnabas said. "In case Cyrus is hurt. He was once a Roman soldier and sometimes acts on instinct."

Macarios nodded, and Barnabas ducked through the entry into the tomb. The floor was covered with broken shards of ossuaries. Barnabas could see the skeleton lying on the shelf in the rear. In the chamber to the left of the skeleton, lamplight fluttered.

28

So as not to spook them, Zarathan cautiously approached the horses. The animals placidly grazed upon the taller grasses growing at the bases of the head-high boulders. The whole slope seemed to be one highly eroded limestone outcrop. He whistled as Cyrus did when he wanted the horse to come, and the big bay lifted his head and pricked his ears. Zarathan whistled again and the horse trotted toward him. The other horse, seeing his friend leaving, let out a short, startled whinny and followed.

"Good boy," Zarathan praised as he gripped the lead rope on Cyrus's horse. It took two tries to catch the rope dangling from the unknown horse's halter.

The horse leaped and tossed its head. Zarathan caught a glimpse of the sheathed sword that hung from the saddle. The ivory hilt gleamed in the dawn light.

"Shh," he soothed. "You're all right, boy. Everything's fine."

The horse stopped twisting, but pawed the ground, throwing up a gray haze of dirt.

As Zarathan turned, he noticed three men as they rode around the southeastern corner of the Temple Mount. When they started down the mountainside, they were silhouetted against the sunrise. They were just dark riders. Zarathan couldn't make out anything about them, but the way they sat their horses sent a surge of fear through him. They were Romans.

Had they been hiding up there?

Zarathan hesitated, uncertain what to do, then led the horses back into the boulders where they'd been grazing.

The riders were negotiating the steep slope as quickly as they could, and appeared to be heading straight for the Shroud Tomb.

"D-did they follow us?"

He glanced at the horsemen, then whirled around to stare to the north, toward the monastery he'd seen being built outside the Damascus Gate. The brothers there must all love Pappas Macarios. Surely he could convince several to ride back with him? But how long would the trip take? How long...

Don't be a fool! Go for help! Now!

Without further consideration, he leaped upon Cyrus's horse, reined it around, and rode flat out for the monastery.

29

Barnabas walked toward the lamp-lit chamber just left of the partially shrouded skeleton. As he neared the doorway, a strange, eerie glow overwhelmed the lamplight. The hair on his arms stood on end as though lightning were about to strike the tomb.

Just as suddenly, the glow faded.

He took two more steps and saw the body on the floor. "Cyrus!"

He ran to kneel beside the man. In the frail lamplight, he could tell very little. Blood had soaked the corpse's hair, making it impossible to judge the original color. "It's not black. It's...lighter. And shorter."

A queer sensation of panic broke inside him. He longed for nothing more than to turn tail and run.

But he rose and walked deeper into the tomb.

"Cyrus? Kalay?" he called loudly.

"Brother Barnabas?" There was a clatter to his right, then a face appeared in a narrow slot near the floor.

"Cyrus!" Joy flooded Barnabas. "You're alive!" Had

he crawled in there to take sanctuary? As the stinging rush of blood began to subside, Barnabas said, "Please tell me Kalay is with you?"

"She is, brother."

"Praise be to God."

"Brother Barnabas?" There was a stunned look in Cyrus's eyes, and his voice...his voice had a low, haunted timbre.

"Cyrus, what's wrong?" Barnabas hurried forward to kneel before the opening. He'd thought at first that it was just another loculus. But now that he could see more clearly, it looked oddly as though it were once a door—a door that had been sealed long ago. The scent that escaped from the chamber was something a man never forgets. The same scent they'd just smelled at the *tekton* tomb...centuries-old air flavored with a hint of spices and aromatic oils that created a tang at the back of the throat.

Inside the chamber, blinding light suddenly blazed and Barnabas flung himself backward with a short cry as he covered his eyes. Icy-blue radiance filled the tomb. As he lowered his shaking hands, he whispered, "What is this?"

As though his words had triggered a silent clap of thunder, another salvo of light burst forth from the opening and dazzling blue fox fire spattered the walls, flickering, dancing, pouring down in glowing serpentine rivulets to puddle on the floor where they pulsed as though alive.

Barnabas couldn't feel his body. He felt as though he were numbly floating off the floor.

"Barnabas?" Cyrus called. "Barnabas, please come over here. Do you know what this is?"

His voice snapped Barnabas from his trance. He got on his hands and knees and crawled through the fox fire to the narrow opening.

In the frosty splendor, Cyrus's bearded face looked unearthly, like an angel's at the moment of creation, pale and shining.

Cyrus stepped aside so that Barnabas could see into the glowing chamber. Kalay stood to the right, near the source of the light, her face invisible in the blue blaze.

"Wait just a moment," Cyrus said. "The light will die down. Or at least it has since we've been here. It seems to come and go at irregular intervals."

Barnabas closed his eyes and watched the streamers on the backs of his lids. When they began to fade, he opened them again.

Kalay came into view, her female figure haloed in glowing blue. Her hair seemed to dance of its own volition.

Dearest Lord God! She's been an angel the entire time!

And then he fixed on the thing resting on the stone table

The sensation of awe that raced through Barnabas could have been no greater if God himself had stepped into the chamber.

In a hoarse whisper, Cyrus asked, "Is this what I think it is?"

Barnabas got down on his stomach and slid partway through the opening, trying to get a better view. The drop was long. He hesitated to jump down, as they had, for fear that his elderly bones would snap on impact.

The skeleton on the table two fathoms below was fully dressed. A large golden ring encircled its right index finger. Even after centuries, the ephod cloth was miraculous. The glittering gold leaf that mixed with the blue, purple, and scarlet threads might have been woven yesterday. But it was the ancient high priest's breastplate—worn over the ephod—that he could not take his eyes from. The twelve translucent stones, rubies, sapphires, opals, and sardonyxes of many colors, each inscribed with the name of a tribe, were the source of the light.[1]

In a trembling voice, Barnabas said, "God always signaled victory in battle by shining those stones."

Astonished, Cyrus said, "Then it is the *essen!* The lost, sacred breastplate of the Essenes?"

"Yes, it must be. Outside of the Ark of the Covenant, this is the most precious sacred artifact in the history of the Ioudaiosoi." Tears blurred Barnabas's eyes. The Truth was sinking in, and with it, awestruck fear. He added, "And he is ours."

Perhaps it was the way Barnabas said *he,* but Cyrus suddenly jerked his head around and stared at the skeleton. He took a small involuntary step forward, then a tortured sound escaped his throat. A heartbeat later, he fell to his knees and clasped his hands in prayer, choking out the words, "Oh, my Lord, my Lord!"

Kalay squinted in disbelief. "It doesn't make sense. Why would Yeshua, an executed criminal, be given the *essen* to wear?"

Barnabas said, "Many saw him as the greatest sage of the time and hoped he would be the military leader promised in the scriptures. Perhaps the Essenes hoped that by giving him the *essen,* he would return to lead them into battle against Rome and win."

"You mean they hoped he was the messiah?"

"Yes." Barnabas tipped his chin to the large, golden ring that encircled the skeleton's finger. "Kalay, is there a symbol on that ring?"

Kalay, still appearing disgruntled, walked around the table and examined it more closely. "It looks like a pomegranate design."

"Yes, that would make sense. The hem of the high priest's robes was embroidered with pomegranate designs, and they were used as the motif for the capitals of Solomon's Temple. The calyx of the fruit also served as a pattern for the crowns of the Torah."

"The *rimonim*," Kalay explained in Hebrew. "Yes, I remem..." Her voice faded, and she frowned.

"What's wrong?"

She gave Barnabas an askance look. "There's a—a scroll. I think. In his hand."

His heart beat louder. "What?"

Kalay gently tugged it from the curled finger bones of the skeleton's left hand. It had been rolled into a tube and tied with what looked like a braid of black hair. "There's something written on the outside of the tube. It's in Hebrew."

Barnabas ordered, "Bring it to me."

When Kalay got to within arm's reach, she handed the narrow papyrus tube up to him.

Barnabas studied the scroll. It was old, fragile beyond belief. Bits of the hair tie cracked off when he touched them and coated his hand. He squinted at the discolored ink. Most of it was impossible to read. Probably the inside was in much better condition. "I can only make out fragments: *Yakob...le...Yos...mati...*"

"From Yakob to Yosef Haramati?" Kalay suggested. "Yeshua's brother Yakob? Are you sure?"

"No, of course not. I'll look at it more closely later. Right now I'm more concerned with him." He gestured to the skeleton.

"Yes, me, too." Kalay's eyes took on a strange, savage glow. "What are you going to do with him? Turn him into a thousand splinters of holy relics? Or respect his beliefs?"

Taken aback by her tone, Barnabas asked, "What do you mean?"

"I mean, stop thinking about yourself. What if he really did believe in the physical resurrection of the body? If you start carrying off pieces of him—"

"Kalay," Barnabas defended, "what ever made you think that I would—"

The clacking sounds of feet shuffling through broken fragments of ossuaries came from the next chamber. Barnabas drew his head from the opening and called, "Zarathan? Macarios? Forgive me, I should have gone to fetch you. I—"

He froze when Macarios entered the lamp-lit chamber with his hands up, followed by Pappas Meridias and his gray-haired henchman.

Quickly, Barnabas tucked the scroll down the front of his robe.

30

The burial chamber went dark. It was as though someone had just blown out a candle—but not before Kalay glimpsed the tall blond bishop she'd first seen in Phoou the morning before the attack on the monastery.

"What happened to the light?" someone gasped.

Barnabas responded, "The wind stirred by your entry must have snuffed the oil lamp."

"Do you take me for a fool?" a man demanded to know. "Lamplight is yellow, not blue! Where did that glow come from?"

Barnabas shifted, and Kalay thought he'd sat up with his back against the entry to conceal as much of it as he could. "Pappas Macarios?" Barnabas called. "Are you well?"

An unknown man answered in a shaky voice, "Yes. They crept up on me outside. I don't know what they—"

"Silence!"

"Pappas Meridias," Barnabas replied, making an

effort to sound calm. "Please, tell us what we may do to help you, and we will do everything in our power—"

"I *knew* you were hiding something!" Meridias said. "What's in here? Is the Pearl here?"

Kalay quietly eased away from the opening, felt for the corner of the table, and edged along it until Cyrus's hand touched hers. Barely audible, he said, "How many men entered the chamber?"

She felt for his face and cupped a hand to his ear to whisper, "I saw three."

"Meridias, Macarios, and another man?"

"Yes, an old man. Gray-headed, but he carried a drawn sword."

"Where was Zarathan?"

She hesitated. He was probably lying dead just outside the tomb. "I didn't see him."

"Kalay, I have to get into that chamber."

"If you grab hold of the ledge right behind Barnabas, when the moment is right, I'll boost you up."

Together they silently eased back to the opening, and Kalay lifted his foot and placed it in the basket she'd made of her knitted fingers. He was heavy; it wouldn't be easy to support his weight. But she had to.

Without warning, the *essen* burst to life. The blue flames flashed and grew into a conflagration that consumed the chamber. Kalay couldn't see anything in that blazing core. Terror emptied her bones, leaving her hollow and frail. As she waited for Cyrus to make his move, she gritted her teeth.

"Get away from that opening!" someone outside ordered. "I want to see what's in there!"

Broken ossuary shards clattered as Barnabas

seemed to sit forward, saying, "Give me a moment. I need to brace my hands. I can't see—"

"Move or you'll be dead!"

Barnabas stood up, and Cyrus hissed, "Now!"

His weight suddenly depressed her hands, and she heaved with all her might.

31

As he lurched through the opening, Cyrus shoved Barnabas to the floor, scrambled to his feet, and charged Meridias before the bishop could react. Driving with all the power in his legs, he collided with Meridias, slamming him into the gray-haired guard. The impact toppled both men to the floor.

"It's Atinius! Kill him, you fool!" Meridias shouted and madly crawled away.

Cyrus leaped for the man, grabbed his sword hand, and bashed it into the floor. The man's grip relaxed, and Cyrus wrenched the sword away, rolled, and came up swinging for Pappas Meridias. The bishop managed to leap back just in time and careened out into the other chamber.

Cyrus lunged after him.

As Cyrus's sword arced toward him, Meridias threw up an arm to protect himself and screamed, "No! Don't!"

The blade gleamed with an edge of pure blue fire as it sliced through Meridias's forearm, hacking off his hand above the wrist; it thudded on the floor, a dead lump of meat.

In shock, Meridias bellowed, "Iesous Christos, save me! Save me!" He grabbed the gushing stump and staggered backward toward the sunlit doorway that led outside, crying, "You'll be damned for eternity for killing me!"

Cyrus hesitated for less than a heartbeat, but it was too long. He felt the keen bite of the dagger pierce his back and heard a low laugh behind him. Stumbling forward, he lifted the sword and spun in an old military maneuver, but his movements were awkward, off-balance. The sicarii easily stepped inside and plunged the dagger into Cyrus's chest. Stunned by the fire, Cyrus froze in disbelief.

The hole in his chest sucked air and spewed blood with each breath he took, telling him it had punctured his right lung. Past the sicarii's head, he saw Barnabas pull Kalay from the hidden doorway and glimpsed her expression as she charged into the room. Roaring like a lion, she leaped on the killer's back just as he drove the dagger into Cyrus again.

"Get off me!" the man shouted and whirled around, trying to throw her off.

"Cyrus, run!" Kalay clawed her fingers into the killer's eyes. The man shrieked as blood spurted over his face.

In panic, the dagger man whipped his knife wildly, trying to strike her in the face. Cyrus mustered his last ounce of strength to bull forward, slamming into the sicarii and knocking both him and Kalay to the floor.

"Kalay, get out of the way!"

Cyrus jumped on the man and wrestled him for the

dagger. He was growing weak. Blood sprayed in a fine mist from his mouth. His body was failing him.

The sicarii ripped the dagger from Cyrus's grip, rolled to his knees, and plunged it once more into Cyrus's chest. The pain was like a bolt of lightning cutting through him. His back arched and he writhed like a fish out of water.

A shadow crossed the chamber outside, and Cyrus glimpsed Zarathan. The boy was shaking so badly he could barely lift the heavy sword in his hands. An incoherent cry ripped from Zarathan's throat as he charged into the chamber.

The stunned guard jerked around and threw up his arm, as though to stop the sharp blade. Zarathan brought it down with all the insane strength in his terrified arms. The keen edge drove through the bone, severing the lower arm, then it cleft the man's skull, and lodged midway through his face.

Zarathan wrenched the sword loose and the body flopped on the floor, spasmed violently, and gradually went still.

"Cyrus?" Kalay ran to him. She used her hands in a vain effort to stop the blood spurting from his chest.

"Oh, dear God, dear God," Barnabas sobbed. Macarios took the old monk in his arms.

Blood frothed at Cyrus's lips as he looked up at Zarathan, and whispered, "Good...good...brother."

Zarathan fixed on his stab wounds. "Oh, forgive me, Cyrus! I—I was afraid to enter the tomb. I rode for the monastery to get help, but turned back. Just...not soon enough."

Kalay said, "Where's Meridias? Did you kill him?"

Zarathan wildly shook his head. "No, he—he fled. I

killed another man who was standing guard outside. Meridias darted past me and blindly ran for the city."

Cyrus coughed up gouts of blood, steadied himself by bracing one hand on the floor, and whispered, "Thank you...brother."

"Cyrus, don't try to speak!" Kalay ordered, but Cyrus wrapped one arm around her and crushed her against him, holding her close, his bloody lips pressed against her red hair. "I love you. I...I needed to tell... you."

Through the gray haze that was filling the chamber, he saw Barnabas and Macarios on their knees, praying... Zarathan weeping.

His heart started fluttering as fast as a bird's, pattering against his ribs, and he couldn't seem to get air into his lungs. He slumped to the floor and rolled onto his back.

His last glimpse was of Kalay. Damp curls of red hair streamed around her beautiful face as she leaned over him. Her cheeks were flushed, and she had a soft, luminous love in her eyes. He kept his gaze on her, fixing on the love...if he could just see her...her love would keep him safe...warm...he wouldn't...

32

The sound of the waves brushing the shore filled the cave.

Barnabas toyed with his chipped wine cup, aimlessly moving it around the table. In the candlelight, the crimson liquid appeared to be alive with golden sparks. His gaze drifted over the codices, scrolls, and papyri in the wall niches, then came back to Libni's face. Graying brown hair straggled around his dark, tear-filled eyes.

Libni whispered, "Was it the *essen?*"

Barnabas heaved a sigh and nodded. "Yes, I think so."

Libni closed his eyes. Tears ran down his cheeks and dripped onto the table where they shone like perfect diamonds. "Are you sure it was him?"

Barnabas sighed. "Many things are possible. I only know that it *felt* like him."

Libni nodded and opened his eyes. As he wiped his face on his sleeve, he said, "It's far more likely that it was a former high priest of the Council, or—"

"Yes, it is."

But as they gazed at each other, Barnabas knew that neither one of them believed that.

Libni leaned forward, his eyes aglow. "Barnabas, do you think that he—"

Voices rose from the tunnel.

Barnabas looked up when Kalay ducked into the chamber. She'd left her long red hair loose; it fell about her shoulders in lustrous waves, highlighting her high cheekbones and full lips. He would always remember her as a blue glowing angel standing beside the long-dead body.

"What is it, Kalay?"

"I just wanted you to know that Zarathan's finally sleeping. Tiras is with him."

Barnabas exhaled a relieved breath. "Thank you."

After they'd fled Jerusalem, Zarathan had taken over Cyrus's role, riding out front, scouting the roads, making certain every place they stopped was safe before they dismounted. He hadn't slept in two days. It was a strange, eerie transformation that Barnabas did not yet understand.

And Kalay...she had barely spoken since Cyrus's death. She, too, had changed. As if the sacred feminine had somehow filled her with its power. She was stronger, more a fortress than any man he had ever known.

"Kalay," Barnabas said, "come and sit down with us. Have a cup of wine."

She ran a hand through her hair, glanced back down the tunnel, then came over and sat at the table.

Libni poured and handed her a cup of wine. "Are you hungry, my dear? I can have Tiras bring food."

She shook her head. "I'm not hungry."

Libni studied her for a long moment with kind eyes, then returned his gaze to Barnabas. "I wouldn't have believed it if I hadn't heard the story from your own lips. I still can't imagine how you had the courage."

Barnabas swirled the wine in his cup, watching the candlelit reflections. "I didn't have any courage. It was Cyrus, Zarathan, and Kalay who were heroic. I just followed the path God set before me."

"Did you hear his voice, as Kalay and Cyrus did?"

He gazed into Libni's wet eyes. "No. If you'd been there, I'm sure you would have heard it. But I did not."

Kalay took a long drink of wine and said, "*If* it was his voice."

Libni smiled his love at her, indulging her disbelief. "What will you do now? Where will you go?"

Barnabas inhaled a deep breath and let it out slowly. "Back to Egypt. There are many rare books there that I buried twenty years ago. It's time I made copies of them and buried them in a variety of places to make sure they survive."

After a time, Libni asked, "And what of Meridias?"

"I assume he lived and returned to Rome, though I have no way of knowing for certain."

"Then Pappas Silvester may know about the Pearl. I assume you took precautions?"

Barnabas wiped his damp palm on his dirty robe. It seemed as though it had been an eternity since he'd bathed or changed clothes. "Meridias never looked into the lower chamber. I don't think he had the slightest idea what was causing the unearthly glow."

Libni stared at Barnabas. "But you know as well as

I, that he'll be back. He'll see it, realize what it is, and destroy—"

"No, he won't," Kalay said. "Nor will he find the books we were carrying with us."

Libni's bushy gray brows drew together. "Then you *did* take precautions? You know what the existence of his body means to Constantine's church?"

"I do. They murdered the monks of my monastery to keep the Truth hidden." Barnabas finished his wine and set his empty cup on the table with a thud. The chips around the rim were sharp and ugly. "Libni...at the Last Supper he told his disciples he would go before them into the Galilaian."[1]

Libni frowned. "Yes, in Markos. I remember."

For a long while, they just gazed into each other's eyes, and a silent communication passed between them, as powerful as it had been in the old days at the library in Caesarea.

Barnabas tapped the side of his cup with a hard fingernail. "Unlike the Church, I respected his wishes."

Libni smiled. Then he chuckled. "Don't tell me," he said as he wiped his tears on his sleeve. "I don't want to know where it is."

Kalay drew her feet up into her chair and propped her wine cup atop her knees. In a soft voice, she asked, "Did you tell Libni about the scroll?"

Libni's head jerked around. "What scroll?"

Barnabas gave Kalay a sour look and hesitated. "Are you sure you want to become involved?"

Ignoring Barnabas's stern expression, Kalay said, "I found it in the hand of the skeleton, as though he'd been clutching it when he died."

"More likely," Barnabas corrected, "it had been

tucked into his dead hand after his body had been prepared."

Libni blinked and straightened in his chair. In a breathless voice, he said, *"You found a scroll in his hand?"*

EPILOGUE

As Pappas Silvester strode down the brazier-lit palace hall, he nervously tugged at his collar; his neck felt swollen, his collar too tight. His fingers came back slick with sweat. He passed several soldiers on guard. Not one looked at him. He might have been a distant insect to them, barely visible.

The deeper he went into the palace, the more the endless columns below the high-arched vaults resembled cold stalagmites. He swore he felt the touch of evil. He had always felt it here, in Constantine's palace. The air grew cold and sinisterly damp. Behind every shadow there lurked a presence, like a living thing, whispering to itself in the darkness.

Or it could have simply been his own fear. At the moment it was slithering around his belly, making him ill.

He rounded a corner and stopped. At the end of the hall, in front of Constantine's chamber, stood four centurions. That was odd. There were always sentries, but he almost never saw men of this rank, or at least, not this many, gathered just outside the emperor's door.

As he walked toward them, the centurions turned.

"A pleasant evening to you, Centurion Felix." Silvester dipped his head. "And Pionius, how are you?" The other two officers, he did not know.

Pionius, a tall, dark-haired man with burly shoulders, answered, "I am well, Pappas. He's waiting for you. *Been* waiting for you. For some time."

In a faintly shrill voice, he cried, "I was only just informed he'd requested me! I hope he's not annoyed."

Pionius extended a hand to the door. "See for yourself."

Pionius and the other officers walked away down the hall, talking in low voices.

Silvester squared his shoulders and, in a small voice, called, "Your Excellency? It's Silvester."

"Enter."

The word carried no hint of anger, which relieved Silvester. He pushed open the heavy door and walked into the chamber.

The emperor sat behind his table, heaped with maps, reading some missive. His brow was furrowed distastefully. He wore a dark-blue cape—threaded through with silver and gold—over a scarlet robe. His sword belt lay across the back of a nearby chair. Easily within reach.

Silvester patiently waited to be recognized. The fire in the hearth cast a flickering amber gleam over the ornately carved furniture and the vaulted ceiling.

Without looking up, Constantine inquired, "Did they find it?"

"Well...er, no. Not exactly."

Constantine's gaze slowly lifted. His eyes were like oiled metal, shiny and hard, capable of ringing eternal darkness. "Answer me."

Silvester flapped his arms against his sides. "Pappas Meridias informed me that they *did* find a tomb with an ossuary marked *Yeshua bar Yosef,* but—"

"And, as I instructed, it was destroyed."

Silvester ran his fingers around his collar again. It was strangling him. "No." He rushed to add, "Because we could not be certain it was *the* ossuary. Pappas Macarios claimed to have *two* more such ossuaries in his office! Apparently the name was extremely common during the time our Lord lived. So, you see, the tomb is no threat to us. We can't prove it is his burial, but *no one else* can prove it either."

Constantine toyed with the missive on his desk, then tossed it aside and stood up. He reached for his sword belt and strapped it on. As he came around the table, Silvester's soul shriveled to nothingness. He had always known that death awaited him here, in this chamber.

Constantine stopped before him, propped his hands on his hips, and said, "I still want the tomb covered over with earth. Bury it deep."

"Yes, Excellency. I'll send word to Pappas Macarios immediately."

Constantine swayed slightly on his feet, as though he'd drunk too much wine while conferring with his centurions.

But when he looked down, there was no hint of drunkenness. The eyes that burned into Silvester were the eyes of an emperor who was at heart also a beast. They were not quite human.

"Silvester, I have spoken with my *strategoi*, my generals, and they agree with me that Christianity, as we have created it, may be the most powerful imperial tool in the history of the empire."

Silvester blinked his confusion. "Excellency?"

"The religion is spreading like a raging forest fire."

"Oh, well, yes, Excellency!" Silvester replied, suddenly excited. "Of course it is! The Truth is like a rare pearl—"

"If we are careful to control and direct the Faith, it will be very useful." He swayed on his feet again, perhaps from exhaustion. "That shouldn't be too difficult now, should it? Without a body, the resurrection is safe."[1]

"Well...we still have enemies. Pappas Eusebios is an advocate of tolerance. He will never willingly submit to our hard-line dogmas. And Pappas Macarios in Jerusalem almost certainly helped the Heretic and his band of thieves. He—"

"There will always be those who oppose us. But when we are finished, only *our* version of the Truth will remain. And, Silvester, I guarantee you, in the end, there will be only *one* pappas of the Church, and he will be in Rome."

The veiled promise that Silvester would one day lead all of Christendom sent a heady rush through him. "But why Rome, Excellency? The other bishops will not be happy."

Constantine turned his back on Silvester and returned to his chair. As he sat down, he extended his hand, palm up, then suddenly closed it to a crushing grip, and hissed, "The Church *will* be mine."

A LOOK AT: BUFFALO JUSTICE
A CONTEMPORARY WESTERN MYSTERY

New York Times bestselling authors W. Michael Gear and Kathleen O'Neal Gear deliver a gripping western filled with murder, corruption, and the battle over the American government's most famous and controversial buffalo herd.

When high-profile conservation lawyer Ryman Banks is gunned down on his own doorstep, Montana Department of Justice Agent Jillian Masterson is assigned to the case. What should be a routine investigation quickly spirals into a deadly web of greed, deception, and bloodshed, all tied to a legal war over the management of Yellowstone's bison. As Jillian digs deeper, she finds herself caught between ruthless power players—corrupt politicians, conservationists with deadly agendas, and a psychotic assassin who will stop at nothing to silence those who stand in the way.

Framed for the crime is Wyoming buffalo rancher John Cody, a man with everything to lose if Yellowstone's bison are declared endangered. As the evidence stacks against him, he races to clear his name while battling an undeniable attraction to the very woman determined to put him behind bars.

But the real killer is still at large...and as Jillian gets closer to the truth, she becomes the next target. With enemies lurking in the shadows and a final showdown looming in a remote Wyoming buffalo corral, Buffalo Justice is a heart-pounding story that will leave you breathless.

AVAILABLE NOW

INTERVIEW WITH
KATHLEEN O'NEAL GEAR
AND W. MICHAEL GEAR

BY K. S. JONES

1. You say that there is an alternate story of the life of Jesus, one that has been suppressed for nineteen centuries. How do you justify that claim? Who suppressed the information?

The Church was involved in a battle to rewrite the "facts" of Jesus's life practically from the beginning, and we find the evidence for this in the ancient documents themselves. Keep in mind that the first scribes who copied the sacred books got them from earlier scribes, who got them from earlier scribes. They were literally copying copies of copies. Mistakes were bound to creep in. A later scribe couldn't read the handwriting of the earlier scribe, so he had to interpret what he thought the letters were. Some scribes were very good, and some were very bad. Later correctors often disagreed with former scribes. In one case, a later scribe, exasperated by changes he found in the fourth-century *Codex Vaticanus,* wrote in the margin, "Fool and knave! Leave the old reading, don't change it!"

The result was that, by the second century, there was a considerable variety of New Testament texts. The manuscripts that are the closest to the original gospels are actually the ones that are the most variable and amateurish. By the time scholars start finding professional, standardized copies, in the fourth and fifth centuries, the gospels had become very different books. Twelve or thirteen verses had been added to the ending of the Gospel of Mark, and an entire chapter to John. There were two dramatically different versions of Matthew, and many individual verses and parables had either been inserted or deleted.

The conspiracy to suppress the information, however, actually begins at the Council of Nicea in 325 C.E. where the New Testament was officially determined. There were hundreds of different gospels circulating at the time, and the council was convened primarily to throw out controversial books, to accept certain versions of the gospels, and establish official Church doctrine. Once the council had determined the official gospels, the Roman Emperor Constantine ordered that the books of "heretics," meaning Christians who held other gospels as sacred, be hunted out and destroyed. He also declared that anyone found copying them would be officially charged with heresy, which was a capital offense punishable by death.

From this point on, the Roman Empire, working with the Church, suppressed the works of anyone who did not agree with the "Official Story." We see this in many places. For example, the Edict of 333 C.E., says:

"Constantine, Victor, Greatest Augustus, to bishops and laity: Arius (presbyter of Alexandria who insisted that since Jesus was indisputably 'begotten,' and therefore 'human.' he must be second to God) having imitated wicked and impious men deserves the same loss of privileges as they. Therefore, just as Porphyry [a Platonist who wrote a detailed work against Christianity] that enemy of piety who put together various illegal works against religion, got his just deserts, so that...his impious books have been obliterated, thus, too, we now order that Arius and those who agree with him shall be called Porphyrians...and if any book written by Arius be found, it is to be consigned to the fire, so that not only his corrupt teachings may vanish, but no memory of him at all may remain."

2. How do you know that twelve or thirteen verses were added to the Gospel of Mark?

We know because of the writings of early Church fathers. For example, Clement of Alexandria and Origen, bishops who lived in the 200s, had no knowledge of verses 9-20 of Mark. By the fourth century, Church historians Eusebius and Jerome wrote that they knew of the longer ending, but also said it was absent from almost all Greek manuscripts they had seen. The earliest Bible, known as the *Codex Sinaiticus*, ends at Mark 16:8. As well, Matthew 16:2, and John 5:4 and 16:24 don't exist. Luke 22:43 is marked as "spurious" by the first of nine correctors who worked on the codex between the fourth and twelfth centuries, but his words were scratched out by the third corrector. The *Sinaiticus* manuscript also includes two books that were sacred to early Christians—the Shepherd of Hermas and the Epistle of Barnabas—that are not in the modern New Testament.

3. So there was a lot of dissention in the early years of Christianity, a lot of disagreements about who Jesus was, and what he taught?

Oh, yes. In the first few decades after his death, April 7th in the year 30, there was a great disagreement about the facts of Jesus's life, and what his teachings were.

New Testament readers are familiar with part of this battle from Galatians, where Paul writes that Galatian Christians were listening to "those who would pervert the Gospel of Christ" (1:7) and believing in a "different gospel" (1:6). That "different" gospel had come from "men of repute in Jerusalem" (2:2) and Paul says that before "certain men came from James" (2:12) Cephas—Peter—had eaten with Gentiles, but after the arrival of "the circumcision party" (2:12), Cephas, Barnabas, and others separated themselves from Gentiles.

Two of the major disagreements of the first and second centuries were over the virgin birth and the bodily resurrection.

4. You claim that Jesus was not born of a virgin. How can you possibly know that?

To start off, remember that only Matthew and Luke use the word "virgin" (*parthenos* in Greek) for Mary, the mother of Jesus. In the case of Matthew 1:23 he was quoting from Isaiah 7:14 where the original Hebrew word was *alma*, which meant simply "young girl." It had none of our modern connotations of being a biological virgin.

Second, if you're searching for the truth, it's very

important to ask what people who did not believe in him had to say about Jesus. And it's also important to ask why certain things were left out of the gospels. For example, the Gospel of John never mentions the name of Jesus's mother. Neither do the epistles of Paul. We have to ask, why not?

We know from the writings of ancient Greek, Roman, and Jewish historians that there a very strong tradition that Jesus was an illegitimate child. For example, in 178 C.E. the Platonist historian Celsus wrote that Mary was pregnant by a Roman soldier named Panthera and was driven away by her husband for adultery. In addition, the Jewish story of Jesus's life, the *Tole-dotli Yeshu,* which contains remnants from the second century, also names Pantera as Jesus's father. And we know from Roman records that Tiberius Julius Abdes Pantera of Sidon served as a Roman archer in Jerusalem from 6 B.C. to 6 C.E. The time period of Jesus' conception and birth.

And the canonical gospels themselves contain references. In John 8:41, when Jesus is sparring with his Jewish critics in Jerusalem they say, "we were not born of fornication!" as if to imply that he was. As well, the noncanonical gospels have many references. In the Gospel of Nicodemus, which dates to the 300s, but probably has origins in the 100s, when Jesus is standing before Pilate, his enemy's charge, "you were born of fornication!" In verse 105 of the Gospel of Thomas, Jesus says, "He who knows the father and the mother will be called the son of a whore."

Also, when Jesus goes to preach in the temple at Nazareth the people call him the "son of Mary." The Jewish people didn't trace descent through the female until after the destruction of the Temple in the year 70. At the time Jesus was in Nazareth descent was traced through the male. To refer to a man as being the son of his mother was gravely offensive. It meant that his paternity was uncertain.

And later gospel writers knew this. So the writers of Matthew, Luke, and John go to great efforts to eliminate this reference. For example, Matthew 12:55 replaces Mary with Joseph, as does John 6:42. Later editors change Mark's words to read things like "the son of the carpenter." The gospel of Mark was often "corrected" by later writers to echo the glosses of Matthew and John.

In fact, the Pantera tradition was so widespread and persistent that early Christians could not simply dismiss it as malicious propaganda. They had to find a place for Pantera. So, for example, in the fourth century, Church father Epiphanius gave Pantera a place in the holy family, claiming that Joseph's father was known as Jacob Pantera. As late as the eighth century attempts were still being made to explain it away, as when John of Damascus writes that Mary's great-grandfather was named Pantera.

5. If Jesus was an illegitimate child, where does the story of Joseph come from?

Again, let's look to the gospels. Mark, the earliest gospel, never mentions Joseph, either directly or indirectly. As well, the Infancy Narratives that name Joseph in Matthew and Luke are problematic. First, they tell different stories. For example, Matthew 1:16, says Joseph's father was Jacob, but Luke 3:23 says his father was Heli. And none of the significant information found in the infancy narratives of either gospel is attested clearly elsewhere in the New Testament. In particular, the following items are found only in the infancy narratives:

1. The virginal conception of Jesus.
2. Jesus's birth at Bethlehem.
3. Herodian knowledge of Jesus's birth and the claim that he was the king. Rather, in Matthew 14:1-2, Herod's son seems to know nothing of Jesus.
4. Wide knowledge of Jesus's birth, since all Jerusalem was startled (Matt. 2:3), and the children of Bethlehem were killed in search of him. Rather, in Matthew 13:54-55, no one seems to know of the marvelous origins of Jesus.
5. John the Baptist is a relative of Jesus and recognized him before his birth (Luke 1:41,44.) But later in Luke 7:19 and John 1:33, John the Baptist seems to have no previous knowledge of Jesus and seems puzzled by him.

What this suggests is that the infancy narratives were once separate elements and were added later to the gospels. They are probably based upon an Old Testament pattern of birth annunciations with stereo-typed features: the appearance of an angel, fear by the visionary, a divine message, an objection by the vision-ary, and the giving of a sign. (For example, the birth of Moses in Exod. 3:2-12 and of Gideon in Judges 6:11-32. For a comparison with Matthew's genealogy, see also Ruth 4:18-22 and 1 Chronicles 1:28, 34, and 2:1-15.)

Many scholars see Matthew's version of the story as a "pre-Matthean narrative associating the birth of Jesus, son of Joseph, with the patriarch Joseph and the birth of Moses." Note also that Joseph, Jesus's "father," like the Old Testament Joseph, had a father named Jacob, went to Egypt, had dreams of the future, was chaste, and was disinclined to shame others, which points to the possibility of there being a "Joseph typology" in Luke 1-2. In other words, using the "Joseph" story was not intended to convey fact, but rather to associate Jesus's birth with other mythic events. Both of the Infancy Narratives seem to be largely products of early Christian reflection on the salvific meaning of Jesus Christ in light of Old Testament prophecies.

In other words, the Infancy Narratives tell us practically nothing about the historical Jesus—nor about his father.

As an aside, many of the early Christian churches used versions of these gospels that did *not* include the Infancy Narratives, probably because they knew they were suspect. This is demonstrated when Theodoret, Bishop of Cyrrhus in Syria, writes about the "heretic" Tatian in 450 C.E.:

"This fellow also composed that gospel called "By the Four," cutting off the genealogies and such other things as show that the Lord was, as for his body, a descendant of David. Not only the adherents of his party used this gospel, but also those who followed the apostolic teaching...I found more than two hundred such books revered in the churches of my own diocese,

and collecting them all, I did away with them and introduced instead the gospels of the four evangelists."

**6. I was intrigued by your analysis of the
Gospel of Mark. You say that the author of
that gospel probably lived in Rome, and that
all the ugly things he** says **about Jews had a
political context. What was going on
politically?**

When Jesus's brother James was murdered sometime between 62-70 C.E., relations within Judaism
began to fall apart, then the Jewish Revolt of 66 cut all
communications with the Mother Church in Jerusalem.
Mark and his community in Rome were suddenly
rudderless. To make matters worse, to the Romans,
Christians *were* Jews. Judaism and Christianity did not
split until around 85 C.E., at exactly the time when the
gospels of Matthew and Luke were being written. To
the Romans, there were Jews who believed the Messiah
had come, and there were Jews who believed the
Messiah had not yet come. The persecution must have
been unbearable. In part, at least, Mark's gospel was
probably a deliberate attempt to shout, "We are not
Jews!" Undoubtedly one of the reasons Mark chose to
vilify Jews in his gospel was that by shifting the blame
for Jesus's death from Rome, where it belonged, to the
Jews, it solved a major public relations problem for
Christians in Rome. It was like saying, "Yes, the Jews
are killing your sons and husbands in Palestine, but they
also killed our Lord. We are *not* Jews! In fact, we hate
Jews as much as you do."

The historical legacy of Mark's vilification,
however, is wrenching. Before the end of the first

century, Christians were forbidden to enter synagogues. By the close of the fourth century, marriages between Jews and Christians were prohibited, and if such marriages occurred, they were treated as adultery. Legislation was promulgated forbidding Jews to prose-lytize, or build new temples, and if a temple had been destroyed, they were forbidden to rebuild it.

His words have, unfortunately, been used to support the murder of millions—though at the time, they were simply self-defense.

7. You mention that the gospels of Matthew and Luke date to around 85 C.E. What do the other gospels actually date to, and who wrote them? We all know they are attributed to Matthew, Mark, Luke, and John, but you say those are made-up names. Who made them up and when?

Yes, the documents themselves are silent as to the names of their authors. During the second century, early Christian scholars attributed the books to Mark, Matthew, Luke, and John, but nowhere in any of the texts is the author cited.

Mark dates to between 68-70 C.E., Matthew to around 80 C.E., Luke dates to 85 C.E., and John to around 100 C.E. The earliest written works that record Jesus's life are actually seven letters from Paul, which date to the 50s and are incorporated in the New Testament. (Scholars generally agree that Romans, 1 and 2 Corinthians, Galatians, Philippians. 1 Thessalonians, and Philemon are genuinely from Paul's hand.) But the first versions of Mark, Matthew, Luke, and John did not appear until after the deaths of James, Peter, and Paul, which occurred just before the destruction of the Temple of 70 C.E.—almost forty years after the death of Jesus.

Incidentally, the oldest surviving New Testament gospel is a 3.4-inch-tall fragment of the Gospel of John that dates to around 125-135 C.E. The earliest copies of the other gospels date to the fourth or fifth centuries.

8. I want to know how you can claim that he did not bodily resurrect from the cross. If he didn't resurrect, what happened to his body?

According to Jewish law, his relatives would have been required to bury him. In the sixteenth century, Rabbi Isaac Luria listed Jesus's burial site in Galilee, just north of Safed, in a graveyard he called, "the burial places of the righteous."

Remember that original version of the earliest gospel, Mark, has no resurrection, nor does the apocryphal Gospel of Thomas. We know that Matthew and Luke, written a decade or two later, include the story of the resurrection. Also, many early Christians did not believe in the resurrection. We know this because early Church leaders like Polycarp, Bishop of Smyrna, 70-156 C.E., wrote an attack against those who "denied the resurrection" by, he says, "perverting the logia of the Lord." Apparently collections of Jesus's sayings and life story that did not include resurrection, probably more than just the gospels of Mark and Thomas, were circulating.

Scholars generally agree that Matthew and Luke used two "gospels" to compose their stories: the Gospel of Mark, which they incorporated almost word for word, and an unknown gospel that scholars refer to as the "Q" document. One of the interesting things about the Q document is that it contains no references to Jesus's miraculous birth or his resurrection. (A good analysis of this can be found in Chapter 3 of Philip Jenkins's book, *Hidden Gospels: How the Search for Jesus Lost Its Way*.)

What seems clear is that there was an early Christian community that saw little significance in the idea of the virgin birth or the resurrection, or had not yet felt the need to invent the stories. They believed that Jesus's significance lay in his words, and his words alone.

9. Give me some examples of undeniable factual errors in the New Testament gospels.

Let's just talk about a few of the obvious errors.

1. Despite what the evangelists record, we know from a wide variety of historical resources that there was no eclipse of the sun during Passover of the year 30. There was an eclipse of the sun during the month of Nisan (April) in the year 33, but it was utterly invisible from Jerusalem. The only solar eclipse visible from Jerusalem during the time period in question occurred on November 24th of the year 29. There were, however, eclipses of the moon on the eve of Passover in the years 30 and 33.

2. The authors of the gospels call Pontius Pilate the "Procurator of Judea." That term is incorrect. Governors were not referred to as Procurators until after the reign of

Claudius in 41 C.E. When Jesus was alive, Pilate was called the "Prefect of Judea," which we know not only from Roman records, but from archaeological inscriptions that date to the period of his rule.

3. The story of Barabbas's release invokes a tradition called the *privilegium paschale* that did not exist in the time of Jesus. Had there been either a Jewish or Roman law establishing such a Passover custom there would be a record of its application either before Jesus, or immediately after him, by some governor, bishop, or priest somewhere. There isn't. Not until the year 367 do we find a Roman law which establishes a custom for pardoning criminals on the feast of Easter, "except for those guilty of sacrilege, adulterers, ravishers, or homicides." So, even in 367 C.E., the convicted murderer, Barabbas, would not have been eligible for release.

4. Luke states that "It happened in those days that a decree went out from Caesar Augustus that the whole world be registered for a tax," but the decree first went out while Cyrenius was governor of Syria. This is the census that leads Joseph and Mary to go to Bethlehem where Jesus was supposedly born. However, we know Cyrenius, which is the Greek form of the name Quirinius, was governor of Syria in 6-7 C.E. We know that the census was held in

6-7 C.E., both from an inscription in
Aleppo in Syria, as well as from Josephus.
There is no other evidence for an empire-
wide census during the reign of Augustus...
so Luke got the date wrong.

Such anachronisms are very important because
they help scholars date the documents.

10. You also say the gospels are wrong, that the Jews could not possibly have tried Jesus on the eve of Passover, just before the crucifixion. Why not?

It was against Jewish law. The Sanhedrin could not try a criminal case in a private house, even the High Priest's house. It was not allowed to try cases at night, or on festival days, or on the eve of festival days—all of which the gospels say happened.

The ignorance of Jewish Law displayed by the authors of gospels is colossal.

11. You claim that the only reason for the Sanhedrin to have held a council meeting that night was to prepare *a defense* for Jesus when he went to trial before Pontius Pilate the next morning. Why would High Priest Kaiaphas, his enemy, do that?

Because there was more at stake than just one man's life. Jesus was, according to all sources, beloved by the people, and certainly some members of the Sanhedrin felt the same way. We know that Joseph of Arimathea and Nicodemus could have been counted upon to defend a beloved Jewish son from the hated Roman oppressors. Pilate had assembled three Roman legions around Jerusalem for Passover, either because he expected trouble or because he wanted to provoke it. The Sanhedrin must have been terrified that Jesus's death would spark a revolt that would result in the destruction of Israel—as Kaiaphas says in John 11:47-48, and history demonstrated that Kaiaphas was right. The insurrection against Rome that began in 66 C.E. ended with the Temple burned, Jerusalem in ashes, and the population decimated and scattered.

Also, consider what the four gospels say. A condemnation (guilty sentence) is found only in Mark 14:64. Matthew 26:66 records that the Sanhedrin "said" he was guilty. Luke 22:71 has the Sanhedrin saying only "what need we of further witnesses." And John deletes the entire trial, probably because he understood Jewish Law better than the other Greek-speaking evangelists.

If the Sanhedrin met that night, it was not to hold court.

12. So you say Jesus was tried under Roman law for a crime against Rome: Treason. Is there any evidence of this trial in the Roman archives? Surely if he'd been so tried Pilate would have had to make a report.

Though Pilate would have been required to make such a report, there isn't one in the Roman archives. The logical explanation is that there was no trial. First of all, a confession would have made a trial unnecessary. Also, Pilate was well known for executing prisoners who had never seen trial. Add to this the fact that Roman historian, Tacitus (55-115 C.E.) writes in his

Annates, 15.44, only that Pilate had Jesus executed. He mentions no trial.

13. You say that the apostle Peter and Mary Magdalen practically hated each other. What's the evidence for that?

We find evidence for it in several noncanonical books, the *Gospel of Philip,* the *Dialogue of the Savior,* the *Gospel of Mary,* and the *Pistis Sophia.* Here are a couple of examples:

1. In the *Gospel of Mary,* after the crucifixion the disciples are terrified and disheartened and ask Mary to tell them what the Savior said to her secretly. When she does, Peter, furious, says: "Did he really speak privately with a woman? . . . Are we to turn about and all listen to her?" Mary, upset by his anger, says, "My brother, Peter, what do you think? Do you think that I thought this up myself in my heart, or that I am lying about the Savior?" At this point Levi breaks in and says, "Peter, you have always been hot-tempered. Now I see you contending against the woman like the adversaries. If the savior made her worthy, who are you to reject her?"

2. In the *Pistis Sophia,* another argument occurs between Mary and Peter. Peter complains that Mary is dominating the conversation with Jesus and displacing the rightful priority of Peter and the other apostles. He urges Jesus to silence her, but

Jesus rebukes him and says that "whoever the Spirit inspires to speak is divinely ordained to speak, whether man or woman." Later, Mary says to Jesus, "Peter makes me hesitate: I am afraid of him because he hates the female race."

3. And in the Gospel of Thomas, Peter says, "Let Mary leave us, for women are not worthy of life."

14. The Gospel of John 18:31 credits Jews with saying to Pilate, "It is not lawful for us to put any man to death...." You say this could not possibly have been said by any Jew with any authority, because it's simply not true. How do you know?

Because the Sanhedrin *did* exercise jurisdiction over capital cases, as is verified by Acts 4:1 -22 and 5:17-42, as well as the historian Josephus in his *Jewish Wars*, 6,2,4.

15. Most people are going to be surprised to discover that Jesus had four brothers and two sisters. What were their names? How do you know they were real brothers and sisters, and not just half siblings, or cousins?

All of the extant original gospels were written in Greek. The Greek word for "brother" is *adelphos*. While the term was often used symbolically, when it applies directly to Jesus, as in Mark 6:3, when the text says that Jesus is the son of Mary and brother (*adelphos*) of James, Joses, Jude, and Simon, it clearly means a physical relationship, not just a symbolic one. In fact, there is no clear case in the New Testament where *adelphos* means stepbrother, stepsister, or cousin. The Greek term for cousin is *anepsios,* and Mark does not call any of these men Jesus's *anepsios.* As well, in both Galatians 1:19, and 1 Corinthians 9:5, Paul uses the term *adelphos,* when he is talking about the brothers of the Lord. Since he uses the term *anepsios* in Col. 4:10, he obviously knew the difference.

This tradition of Jesus having real brothers and sisters was kept alive by at least some Church leaders up until the fourth century, when Mary's perpetual virginity was established as Church dogma.

16. You say that in 135 c.e., Golgotha, the location of the tomb of Jesus, became a landfill, and was covered over by a statue to Aphrodite. Who did that and why? Were they trying to destroy the tomb of Jesus?

After the Bar Kokhba rebellion, which lasted from 132 to 135 c.e., Emperor Hadrian, who was trying to destroy the Jews and everything they cherished, changed the name of Jerusalem to Colonia Aelia Capitolina, and as part of the construction of the city turned the *Kraniou Topon,* the Place of the Skull, into a vast landfill upon which he built a Temple to Aphrodite.

And that was not the only time the sacred Christian sites were assaulted. In the year 303, Emperor Diocletian ordered the destruction of all Christian churches and texts.

17. Disagreements in the New Testament

gospels created a big controversy over the date of Easter, didn't they?

Yes, this was a very difficult subject in early Christianity. In Asia Minor, Easter was celebrated on the Jewish Passover (Pesach), that being the date of the crucifixion in the Gospel of John. But Matthew, Luke, and Mark make the Last Supper the Passover meal, and place the crucifixion a day later. In the 150s Polycarp of Smyrna visited Rome to discuss this issue, but no agreement could be reached. Rome insisted upon celebrating Easter on the Sunday following the first full moon after the spring equinox, and nothing was going to change its mind. In the 190s Bishop Victor of Rome was so upset that the churches in Asia Minor celebrated Easter on the Jewish Passover that he threatened to excommunicate anyone who did not adopt the Roman date. In the mid third century Bishop Stephen of Rome got into a vehement argument over this subject with Bishop Cyprian of Carthage, who had the support of the Greek East. It was the first occasion on which the Bishop of Rome is known to have invoked Matthew 16:18 to justify the primacy of Rome. This disagreement would be one of the lasting disputes between the Eastern Church and the Western Church.

18. You footnoted your novel. Isn't that a little unusual? I mean, fiction is fiction, right?

Yes, and no. In all of our books we use the best nonfiction information available to re-create the past. With this book, we felt it was especially important to footnote our sources. People have a right to know where the information comes from.

19. You are both archaeologists. You must have known that this book would stir up a lot of controversy. Why did you want to write *The Betrayal* and *The Tomb*?

Because over the centuries the myth of Jesus has so obscured the actual facts of his life that his true story has been lost. Knowledge does not destroy faith. It does not take Jesus away. In fact, it can restore the profound meaning of his life that has been stolen by centuries of revisionism.

ABOUT W. MICHAEL GEAR

W. Michael Gear is a *New York Times, USA Today,* and international bestselling author of sixty novels. With close to eighteen million copies of his books in print worldwide, his work has been translated into twenty-nine languages.

Gear has been inducted into the Western Writers Hall of Fame and the Colorado Authors' Hall of Fame —as well as won the Owen Wister Award, the Golden Spur Award, and the International Book Award for both Science Fiction and Action Suspense Fiction. He is also the recipient of the Frank Waters Award for lifetime contributions to Western writing.

Gear's work, inspired by anthropology and archaeology, is multilayered and has been called compelling, insidiously realistic, and masterful. Currently, he lives in northwestern Wyoming with his award-winning wife and co-author, Kathleen O'Neal Gear, and a charming sheltie named, Jake.

ABOUT KATHLEEN O'NEAL GEAR

Kathleen O'Neal Gear is a *New York Times* bestselling author of fifty-seven books and a national award-winning archaeologist. The U.S. Department of the Interior has awarded her two Special Achievement awards for outstanding management of America's cultural resources.

In 2015 the United States Congress honored her with a Certificate of Special Congressional Recognition, and the California State Legislature passed Joint Member Resolution #117 saying, "The contributions of Kathleen O'Neal Gear to the fields of history, archaeology, and writing have been invaluable..."

In 2021 she received the Owen Wister Award for lifetime contributions to western literature, and in 2023 received the Frank Waters Award for "a body of work representing excellence in writing and storytelling that embodies the spirit of the American West."

SELECTED BIBLIOGRAPHY

Adkins, Roy and Lesley, *Dictionary of Roman Religion*. New York: Facts on File, 1996.

Barnstone, Willis, ed., *The Other Bible*. New York: HarperCollins, 1994.

Barton, John, *The Biblical World*, vols. 1-2. New York: Routledge, 2002.

Ben-Dov, Meir, *Historical Atlas of Jerusalem*. New York: Continuum, 2002.

Betteson, Henry, *The Early Christian Fathers*. London: Oxford University Press, 1969.

--. *The Later Christian Fathers*. London: Oxford University Press, 1970.

Boring, M. Eugene, et al., eds., *Hellenistic Commentary to the New Testament*. Nashville: Abingdon Press, 1995.

Borret, M., ed., *Origene, Contre Celse. Tome I (Livres I et II)* SC 132; Paris: Cerf, 1967.

Brandon, S.G.F., *Jesus and the Zealots*. New York: Charles Scribner's Sons, 1967.

Brooten, Bernadette, *Women Leaders in the Ancient Synagogue*. Brown University, Brown Judaic Studies, Number 36. Atlanta: Scholars Press, 1982.

Brown, Raymond E., *An Introduction to the New Testament*. New York: Doubleday, 1997.

Brunier, Serge, and Jean-Pierre Luminet, *Glorious Eclipses: Their Past, Present, and Future*. Cambridge: Cambridge University Press, 2000.

Carroll, James, *Constantine's Sword*. New York: Houghton Mifflin, 2001.

Cohen, Shaye J. D., "Was Timothy Jewish (Acts 16: 1-3)? Patristic Exegesis, Rabbinic Law, and Matrilineal Descent," *Journal of Biblical Literature*, 105 (1986). pp. 251-68.

Cohn, Haim, *The Trial and Death of Jesus*. Old Saybrook, Connecticut: Konecky and Konecky, 1963.

Charlesworth, James H., *Jesus and the Dead Sea Scrolls*. London: Doubleday, 1992.

Codex Justinianus and *Digesta*. English translation (*Corpus Juris Civilis*) by Scott, 1931.

Codex Theodosius. English translation by Pharr, 1952.

Coogan, Michael D., *The Oxford Illustrated History of the Biblical World*. Oxford: Oxford University Press, 1998.

Dart, John, *The Jesus of Heresy and History: The Discovery and Meaning of the Nag Hammadi Gnostic Library*. San Francisco: Harper and Row, 1988.

Doresse, Jean, *The Secret Books of the Egyptian Gnostics*. Rochester, Vermont: Inner Traditions International, 1986.

Dungan, David Laird. *A History of the Synoptic Problem: The Canon, the Text, the Composition, and the Interpretation of the Gospels*. New York: Doubleday, 1999.

Edersheim, Alfred, *The Temple: Its Ministry and Services*. Peabody, Massachusetts: Hendrickson Publishers, 1994.

Ehrman, Bart D., *Lost Christianities: The Battles for Scripture and the Faiths We Never Knew*. Oxford: Oxford University Press, 2003.

--. *Lost Scriptures: Books That Did Not Make It into the New Testament*. Oxford: Oxford University Press, 2003.

--. *Misquoting Jesus: The Story Behind Who Changed the Bible and Why*. New York: HarperCollins, 2005.

--. *Peter, Paul, and Mary: The Followers of Jesus in History and Legend*. Oxford: Oxford University Press, 2006.

Epstein, Isidore, ed., *The Babylonian Talmud: Seder Nezikin in Four Volumes*. English translation by Jacob Shachter. London: Soncino, 1935.

Eusebius. *Historia Ecclesiastica*. New York: Penguin, 1965.

Filoramo, Giovanni, *A History of Gnosticism*. Cambridge: Basil Blackwell, 1991.

Fredriksen, Paula, *From Jesus to Christ: The Origins of the New Testament Images of Jesus*. New Haven: Yale University Press, 1988.

Freedman, David Noel, ed., *The Anchor Bible Dictionary*, vols. 1-6. New York: Doubleday, 1992.

Galambush, Julie, *The Reluctant Parting: How the New Testament's Jewish Writers Created a Christian Book*. New York: HarperCollins, 2005.

Hadas-Lebel, Mireille, *Flavius Josephus: Eyewitness to Rome's First-Century Conquest of Judea*. New York: Macmillan, 1993.

Haskins, Susan, *Mary Magdalen: Myth and Metaphor*. New York: Harcourt Brace, 1993.

Hatch, William Henry Paine, *The Principal Uncial Manuscripts of the New Testament*. Chicago: University of Chicago Press, 1939.

Hull, John M., *Hellenistic Magic and the Synoptic Tradition: Studies in Biblical Theology*, second series, 28. London: SCM Press, 1974.

James, M. R., *The Apocryphal New Testament*. Oxford: Oxford University Press, 1980.

Jenkins, Philip, *Hidden Gospels: How the Search for Jesus Lost Its Way*. Oxford: Oxford University Press, 2001.

Martin, Raymond A., *Studies in the Life and Ministry of the Historical Jesus*. New York: University Press of America, 1995.

McManners John, ed., *The Oxford Illustrated History of Christianity*. Oxford: Oxford University Press, 1990.

Meier, John P., *A Marginal Jew: Rethinking the Historical Jesus*, vols. 1-3. New York: Doubleday, 1994.

Metzger, Bruce, and Michael Coogan, *The Oxford Companion to the Bible*. Oxford: Oxford University Press, 1993.

Meyer, Marvin, and Richard Smith, *Ancient Christian Magic-Coptic Texts of Ritual Power*. San Francisco: HarperCollins, 1994.

Meyers, Carol, *Discovering Eve: Ancient Israelite Women in Context*. Oxford: Oxford University Press, 1988.

Nestle-Aland, *Novum Testamentum, Graece*. London: United Bible Societies, 1971.

Neusner, Jacob, *Introduction to Rabbinic Literature*. New York: Doubleday, 1994.

Oden, Thomas, ed., *Ancient Christian Commentary on Scripture*, vols. I—IX. Illinois: InterVarsity Press, 2001.

Pagels, Elaine, *The Gnostic Gospels*. New York: Random House, 1989.

Pagels, Elaine, and Karen King, *Reading Judas: The Gospel of Judas and the Shaping of Christianity*. New York: Penguin, 2007.

Philo, Alexandrinus, *Legatio ad Gaium*. Edited by E. Mary Smallwood. Leiden: E. J. Brill. 1961.

Qualls-Corbett, Nancy, *The Sacred Prostitute*. Toronto: Inner City Books, 1988.

Richardson, Peter, *Herod: King of the Jews and Friend the Romans*. Columbia: University of South Carolina Press, 1996.

Riley, Gregory J., *Resurrection Reconsidered: Thomas and John in Controversy*. Minneapolis: Fortress Press, 1995.

Robinson. James M. *The Nag Hammadi Library in English*. San Francisco: Harper and Row, 1988.

SELECTED BIBLIOGRAPHY

Rudolph, Kurt, *Gnosis: The Nature and History of Gnosticism*. San Francisco: Harper and Row, 1987.

Schaberg, Jane, *The Illegitimacy of Jesus*. Sheffield: Sheffield Academic Press, 1995.

Schonfield, Hugh, *The Essene Odyssey: The Mystery of the True Teacher and the Essene Impact on the Shaping of Human Destiny*. Rockport: Element Books, 1993.

Shanks, Hershel, and Ben Witherington, *The Brother of Jesus*. New York: HarperCollins, 2003.

Smith, Morton, *Jesus the Magician*. San Francisco: Harper and Row, 1978.

Suetonius, Gaius, *De Vita Caesarum*. New York: Penguin, 1957.

Tabor, James D., *The Jesus Dynasty*. New York: Simon & Schuster, 2006.

Tacitus, Cornelius, *Annales*. New York: Penguin, 1962.

Thiering, Barbara, *Jesus and the Riddle of the Dead Sea Scrolls: Unlocking the Secrets of His Life History*. San Francisco: HarperCollins. 1992.

Toner, J. P., *Leisure and Ancient Rome*. Oxford: Black well Publishers, 1995.

Torjesen, Karen Jo, *When Women Were Priests*. San Francisco: HarperCollins, 1993.

Ulrich, Eugene, *The Community of the Renewed Covenant: The Notre Dame Symposium on the Dead Sea Scrolls*. Notre Dame: University of Notre Dame Press, 1994.

Vermes, Geza, *The Complete Dead Sea Scrolls in English*. New York: Penguin, 1997.

Wainwright, Geoffrey, and Karen B. Westerfield Tucker, *The Oxford History of Christian Worship*. Oxford: Oxford University Press, 2006.

Whiston, William, *The Genuine and Complete Works of Flavius Josephus*. Dublin: Thomas Morton Bates, 1796.

ENDNOTES

INTRODUCTION

1. The gospels contained in our modern New Testament were written decades after the events they describe. The Gospel of Mark, probably written in Rome, is the earliest gospel, dating to around 68-70 c.e: Matthew and Luke clearly relied upon Mark's gospel, incorporating it into their own gospels without substantial changes. Matthew was likely composed in Antioch, the capital of Syria, and dates to around the year 80. The writings of Luke, who authored not only the Gospel of Luke and the Acts of the Apostles, but also probably the Pastoral Letters attributed to Paul, date to 80-85. The Gospel of John was the latest to be written, dated to around 100-110 c.e., though some scholars argue for an earlier date, 90-95.

   And let us be clear, the actual authors of the gospels are unknown. The documents themselves are silent as to the writers' identities. During the second century, early Christian scholars attributed the texts to Mark, Matthew, Luke, and John, but nowhere in the texts is the author cited. As well, our current New Testament gospels were not the earliest versions of those gospels. The oldest surviving papyrus of any gospel, known as the Rylands Papyrus, is a 3.4-inch-tall Greek fragment of the Gospel of John that dates to around 125-35 c.e. The earliest copies of the other gospels date to the fourth or fifth centuries. We know that over time the gospels underwent dramatic editing, and there is good evidence that the evangelists invented or interpreted the stories to make them relevant to their place and time. John, for example, originally ended at chapter 20. An early editor clearly didn't like John's ending, so he created a new one. This is made clear by the fact that the additional chapter, which immediately follows, arrives at a completely different conclusion than the original ending. (For more on this see Galambush, pp. 284-86.)

   In addition, virtually every scholar agrees that the earliest versions of the Gospel of Mark end at 16:7 or 16:8. Clement of Alexandria and Origen, two of the earliest Church scholars who lived in the 200s, had no knowledge of verses 9-20. In the fourth century, Eusebius and Jerome knew of the existence of this longer ending, but also said it was absent from almost all Greek manuscripts they had seen. In the oldest known Bible, the fourth-century "Sinaiticus" document, the women find the tomb empty and are told by a man in white that he has risen. They run away in terror. The gospel ends, simply, with an empty tomb. There is no resurrection, and no "sightings" of Jesus.

The longer ending of Mark was probably added in the fourth century, probably by a pious scribe who was copying Mark and decided he needed a more dramatic ending, one akin to the endings of Matthew and Luke. Verses 9-20 were not the only "other" endings of Mark, either. Two more invented endings were also circulated in the early years of the faith. Both were shorter versions.

But do not mistake this historical analysis to mean that early Christians did not believe in the resurrection or the post-crucifixion sightings of Jesus. Some certainly did, as the letters of Paul, dated to the 50s, document—though it's clear Paul believed in a spiritual resurrection, not a bodily resurrection—but there was a great argument about these issues among early Christians.

For a more lengthy discussion of these subjects, please review the entries under the evangelists' names in *The Anchor Bible Dictionary* edited by David Noel Freedman, and also see Tabor, pp. 230-33.

CHAPTER 2

1. The Gospel of Philip, 73:22-23.
2. The Gospel of Nicodemus, chapters XII-XIII.

CHAPTER 3

1. While Jews were not allowed to return to Jerusalem after the siege in the year 70, Christians were. Christians were at first expelled along with Jews, but were permitted to return a few years later because they proclaimed they were not part of the Jewish community, and said they welcomed the destruction of the Temple as the fulfillment of Jesus's prophecies. They were allowed to resettle the Mount Zion portion of the city. For more on this, see Meir Ben-Dov's *Historical Atlas of Jerusalem*, pp.

142-52, and the *Anchor Bible Dictionary* entry for "Temple-Jerusalem."

Jews were finally given permission to return to Jerusalem in the year 362. The new emperor, who would become known as Julian the Apostate, gladly allowed Jews to return to Jerusalem. He hated Christianity. Right after he decreed the end of the Christian empire, he ordered the Jewish Temple rebuilt in Jerusalem. To place "one stone upon another" was—in Julian's mind—to conquer the false messiah. He reigned for less than two years, dying during a failed invasion of Persia. More prophetic to Christians was the fact that Jews excavating the new foundation of the Temple touched off mighty explosions of gaseous deposits, which ended the last attempt to rebuild the Temple. Christians. naturally, saw this as the miraculous intervention of God. (See more on this in Carroll, pp. 205-207.)

2. These are the oral legends that circulated at the time of the Council of Nicea. The best recommendation for all matters pertaining to Constantine is James Carroll's book *Constantine's Sword*. For more on his political agenda. see pp. 191-93.

CHAPTER 4

1. Yes, the Square of the Column is real. See Meir Ben-Dov, *Historical Atlas of Jerusalem*, p. 120.

CHAPTER 6

1. Most scholars hold that the probable location for Pilate's Praetorium is Herod's Upper Palace along the western wall of the city. We do not agree. There is a total lack of any early Christian tradition regarding that location. The earliest Christian writings say that the Praetorium stood near the western slope of the Tyropoeon valley, opposite the southwest corner of the Temple Mount. In 333 c.e., the Anonymous of Bordeaux, who provides us with the earliest pilgrim account, reported that the crumbling walls of the Praetorium faced the Tyropoeon valley, and in 450 c.e. a church was built on the site. If early Christian tradition is correct, the only thing that could have stood in these locations was the ancient royal palace of the Hasmoneans.

2. Judge Haim Cohn's analysis of Roman law as it applied to the trial of Jesus before Pilate is fascinating reading, pp. 142-90.

3. In rabbinic literature the evidence for the term "rabbi" as a mode of address prior to the year 70 is scant. Before 70, men were apparently not referred to by the title "rabbi" (e.g. Hillel, Shammai), but after 70, they were. For example, Rabbi Aquiba. Though Luke does not use the term "rabbi" for Jesus, Matthew does, and it is apparently polemical, since Judas is the only person who calls Jesus "rabbi." Mark and John also call Jesus "rabbi." But these usages are probably anachronistic. After all, the gospels were written just before or after the year 70. We know of one literary reference in the period before 70 c.e. where *rab* is used to designate a teacher (*t. Pesah.* 4.13-14), and there is one ossuary in Jerusalem that also dates to around this time period that is inscribed rab hana. We have, as a result, chosen to use the term *Rab* in the same way that one would say "teacher." For a more detailed discussion on this, please see Meier, vol. 1, pp. 119-20.

4. The silence of Jesus before the Sanhedrin and Pilate has been seen as a fulfillment of Isaiah 52:13-53:12. Whether or not Jesus deliberately intended to play the role of the Isaianic servant by remaining silent "as a sheep before her shearers is dumb, so he openeth not his mouth" (KJV), or whether he was obeying the Jewish custom of proper behavior when insulted, we cannot say. But Jesus undoubtedly knew these passages very well.

5. There is no report of Jesus's trial in the imperial archives of Rome, though Pilate would have been required to make such a report. (See M. Craveri, *The Life of Jesus,* p. 392.)

   Does that mean there was no trial? It may. After all, a "confession" would have made an official trial unnecessary. Also, there is a letter quoted by Philo, a contemporary of Yeshua's, regarding Pilate. In his *De Legatione ad Gaium,* Philo quotes a letter from King Agrippa I to Emperor Caligula, which describes Pilate's government as characterized by "his venality, his violence, his thefts, his assaults, his abusive behavior, his frequent executions of untried prisoners and his endless savage ferocity." Pilate was well known for executing prisoners who had never seen trial. Add to this the fact that the Roman historian Tacitus (c. 55-115 c.e.) writes in his *Annales,* 15:44, only that Pilate had Jesus executed. He mentions no trial.

6. The date was Nisan the 14th, or, by our calendar, April 7, the year 30. See Meier, *A Marginal Jew,* vol. 1, pp. 401-02. Keep in mind that at around 7:00 p.m. that night the date changed to Nisan the 15th, and Passover began. If Jesus "rose" on Sunday, it had technically only been two and a half days.

7. Joseph of Arimathea, a scholar of the law, and a pious Jew, would certainly have requested the bodies of any fellow Jew who died that day—if for no other reason than to obey Jewish law.

8. Digesta, 48,24,1, and Tacitus, *Annates*, 6,29.

9. M Sanhedrin VI 5.

10. Under Roman law, a crucified man could not be buried. Under Jewish law convicts executed by order of the Roman prefect had to, eventually, be buried and mourned according to Jewish tradition (Semahot II 7 and 11). As Cohn notes on p. 239, "That it was a Roman court which had sentenced him was enough to entitle him to the benefits of Jewish burial and traditional Jewish mourning."

11. You may be wondering why we did not use the story of Barabbas's release. This tradition, called the *privilegium paschale*, did not exist at the time of Jesus. Had there been either a Jewish or Roman law establishing such a custom, there would be a record of its application, either before the life of Jesus or after, by some governor, bishop, or priest, somewhere. There isn't. Not until the year 367 do we find a Roman law, the *indulgentia criminum*, which establishes a custom for pardoning criminals on the feast of Easter, except for those "guilty of sacrilege against the Imperial Majesty, of crimes against the dead, sorcerers, magicians, adulterers, ravishers, or homicides." Even in 367, then, Barabbas, the convicted murderer, would not have been eligible for release. As well, only the emperor himself could grant a pardon under the *indulgentia criminum*. Provincial governors did not have the right to do so. Such an act would have been seen as usurping imperial prerogative, and tantamount to treason. Lastly, there is no evidence that the emperor granted "special" dispensation to Pilate to allow him to grant such pardons to curry the favor of the Jews. Nor, we must conclude, would Pilate have done so if he'd had the right to. Pilate was notorious in his contempt for Jews.

This is another example of the gospel writers' attempts to make Jews appear to be the culprits, rather than Rome. Keep in mind the political context at the time the gospels were being written. Jerusalem was about to be, or had just been, attacked and destroyed. Romans had issued a decree forbidding Jews from even visiting the city, let alone living there, and left the Tenth Legion in the city to enforce the decree. Christians had begged the commanders of the legion to allow them back into the city, claiming they were not part of the Jewish community, and saying they were happy Rome had destroyed the Temple. The commanders, who needed civilians to provide services for their troops, and were probably happy to work with the enemies of the Jews, agreed. Christians were allowed to return to Jerusalem. Relations between Jews and Christians became extremely volatile, so much so that Judaism and Christianity finally split around 85 C.E.—the exact time when the gospels of Matthew and Luke were being written. (For more on this see Meir Ben-Dov's *Historical Atlas of Jerusalem*, pp. 136-42, and *The Oxford Illustrated History of Christianity*, edited by John McManners, pp. 21-26, and especially Brandon, pp. 2-4 and pp. 262-76.)

Also, try to imagine what it must have been like to be a Christian in Rome, as Mark probably was, after the start of the Jewish War in the year 66. When James was murdered in 62, relations with Judaism began to fall apart, then the revolt of 66 cut all communications with the mother church in Jerusalem. Mark and his community were suddenly rudderless. To make matters worse, to the Romans, Christians *were* Jews. There was no such thing as "Christianity." There were Jews who believed the messiah had come, and they called themselves Christians, but the sect was part of Judaism. The persecution must have been unbearable. In part, at least, Mark's gospel was probably a deliberate attempt to shout, "We are not Jews!" Undoubtedly one of the reasons Mark chose to vilify Jews in his gospel was that by shifting the blame for Jesus's death from Rome—where it belonged—to the Jews, it solved a major public relations problem for Christians in Rome. It was like saying, "Yes, the Jews are killing your sons and husbands in Palestine, but they also killed our Lord. We hate Jews as much as you do."

The historical legacy of Mark's vilification is wrenching—his words have been used to support the murder of millions. But at the time, it was likely just self-defense.

S.G.F. Brandon's chapter entitled "The Markan Gospel," in his book *Jesus and the Zealots,* is very valuable for a better understanding of this issue.

Keep in mind, also, that before the end of the first century, Christians were forbidden to enter synagogues. By the close of the fourth century, marriages between Jews and Christians were prohibited, and if such marriages occurred, they were treated as adultery. Legislation was promulgated forbidding Jews to proselytize, or build new synagogues. (Coogan, pp. 582-87.)

The first few centuries were horrifying—for both sides—and it got worse.

CHAPTER 9

1. The Gospel of Thomas, verse 24.

CHAPTER 12

1. The city of Emmaus is another mystery to scholars. In his *Onomastican* (90:16) Eusebios identifies it as the city of Nicopolis. However, in 440 Hesychius of Jerusalem said that Nicopolis was too far from Jerusalem to be the Emmaus listed in Luke 24. Other sites have been recommended by scholars, including el-Qubeibeh, and Abu Ghosh, Qaloniyeh. In his *Antiquities* (Book XVIII, chapters 2, 3) however, Josephus says that Emmaus is a "little distance" from the city of Tiberias in Galilee.
2. Luke 24:13.
3. There has been great speculation about the identity of the unnamed apostle who accompanied Cleopas that day outside Emmaus (see the *Anchor Bible Dictionary* entry for "Cleopas"). The main scholarly choices include Peter, Nathaniel, Deacon Philip, Nicodemus, Simon, and many others. We leave you to make your own choice, as we have.

CHAPTER 13

1. A good reference here is *The Oxford History of the Biblical World,* edited by Michael Coogan, pp. 567-69.
2. For pictures of these artifacts, see Ben-Dov's *Historical Atlas of Jerusalem,* p. 139.

CHAPTER 14

1. What Jesus actually said on the cross has been a subject of heated debate for almost two thousand years. This saying is found only in Mark and Matthew. The controversy stems from the fact that the words recorded by Mark and Matthew are not Greek, Hebrew, or Aramaic. Mark's version, *Eloi, Eloi, lama sabachthani,* which is written in Greek, is at best a "Hebraized" transliteration of Aramaic that is probably an attempt to make

Jesus appear to be quoting Ps. 22:1. Two early manuscripts of Mark read *zaphthani*, rather than *sabachthani*, which is at least closer to the Hebrew. In addition, many of the ancient Latin translators couldn't bring themselves to translate the nonsense word *sabachthani* as "forsaken," so that we find they substituted *exprobasti me* (you have tested me), or *me in opprobrium dedisti* (you have given me over to hatred), and even *meledixisti* (you have wished me ill). The apocryphal Gospel of Peter reads *he dunamis mou* (my Power) for "My God," and *kateleipsas me* (you have left me behind), rather than *egkatelipes me* (you have forsaken me).

For more information, see *Mark: A New Translation with Introduction and Commentary*, by C. S. Mann, pp. 650-51.

2. Despite what the evangelists record, we know from a wide variety of historical and astronomical resources that there was no eclipse of the sun during Passover of the year 30. There was an eclipse of the sun during the month of Nisan in the year 33, but it was utterly invisible from Jerusalem. The only solar eclipse visible from Jerusalem during the time period in question occurred on November 24 of the year 29. The Greek historian Phlegon mentions this event in his *History of the Olympiads,* and notes that it was accompanied by an earthquake. There were, however, eclipses of the moon on the eve of Passover in the years 30 and 33. A good discussion of the astronomical events surrounding the crucifixion can be found in *Glorious Eclipses: Their Past, Present, and Future,* by Serge Brunier and Jean-Pierre Luminet.

3. M Shabbat VI 10; B Shabbat 67a; J Shabbat VI 9; Maimonides, Mishneh Torah, Hilkhot Shabbot 6,10; Plinius, *Historia Naturalis,* 28, 36. In addition, Haim Cohn's chapter entitled "The Crucifixion," pp. 219-21, is essential reading for anyone interested in the legal and cultural traditions of both the Jews and Romans.

CHAPTER 15

1. This is partly based on the real Tomb of the Shroud located in the Hinnom valley just outside the old city walls of Jerusalem. Ossuaries labeled mari and salome were found there, as well as the shrouded skeleton described in this novel. See Tabor's *The Jesus Dynasty,* pp. 1-21, for more information.

CHAPTER 20

1. The Gospel of Mary, 17 and 18.

CHAPTER 23

1. According to the Gospel of Nicodemus XV, Joseph of Arimathea was questioned by Kaiaphas and Annas. His answers make great reading.

CHAPTER 24

1. This tomb also exists. It's better known as the Talpiot Tomb, also south of the old city walls of Jerusalem in East Talpiot (see Tabor, pp. 22-33). Anyone familiar with the ossuaries in this tomb will note that we have slipped the famous James ossuary into the Talpiot Tomb. This is not purely artistic license. The Talpiot Tomb was discovered in 1980. When you read Amos Kloner's original archaeological report, it notes that ten ossuaries were recovered during the excavation. The tenth ossuary was given accession number IAA:80.509, which means it was cataloged, along with the other artifacts, by the Israel Antiquities Authority. However, in 1994 the State of Israel published a catalog of the ossuaries from the Talpiot Tomb and listed only nine. The tenth ossuary was mysteriously missing. James Tabor recently noted that the dimensions of the missing ossuary, 60 by 26 by 30 centimeters, exactly match those of the James ossuary. This by no means proves that the *James* ossuary was originally found in the Talpiot Tomb—but it's an interesting possibility.

CHAPTER 25

1. There really are two other *Jesus son of Joseph* ossuaries known in Israel. The first was first written about in 1931 by E. L Sukenin of the Hebrew University (it was purchased by the Palestine Archaeological Museum, 1926). This ossuary is inscribed twice. One inscription says simply *Yeshu*, the other inscription reads *Yeshua bar Yehosef. Yehosef* is another spelling of "Joseph." The second ossuary has one inscription: *Yeshua bar Yehosef*. (See Shanks and Witherington, *The Brother of Jesus*, pp. 58-60.) One of the most interesting references that uses this name is found in

the Cave of Letters at Nahal Hever, seven miles north of Masada. The document says that a woman named Babata married Yeshua ben Yosef, and that their son was named Yeshua (Meier, vol. 1, p. 357).

All this proves is that the name "Jesus son of Joseph" was very common.

2. Shanks and Witherington, pp. 56-59.

CHAPTER 29

1. This description comes from "The Hymn of the Pearl," a narrative poem about a savior who must himself be saved. This beautiful fable of redemption is probably pre-Christian and pre-Gnostic.

CHAPTER 32

1. Mark 14:28. There is a grave of *Yeshu ha Notzri,* Jesus of Nazareth, in Galilee. It's just north of Tsfat (Safed). Few people know about it. Almost no one visits it.

In the sixteenth century, the Kabbalistic rabbi Isaac ben Luria listed this grave along with the graves of other Jewish sages and saints, calling them "the burial places of the righteous."

EPILOGUE

1. On the issue of the resurrection, we recommend Gregory J. Riley's book *Resurrection Reconsidered: Thomas and John in Controversy.*